REYNOLDS RESTORATION

# FULL THROTTLE

–5–

*NEW YORK TIMES* AND *USA TODAY* BESTSELLING AUTHOR
# MELANIE MORELAND

Dear Reader,

Thank you for selecting Full Throttle to read. Be sure to sign up for my newsletter for up to date information on new releases, exclusive content and sales. You can find the form here: https://bit.ly/MMorelandNewsletter

Before you sign up, add melanie@melaniemoreland.com to your contacts to make sure the email comes right to your inbox! **Always fun - never spam!**

My books are available in paperback and audiobook! You can see all my books available and upcoming preorders at my website.

The Perfect Recipe For **LOVE**
xoxo,
Melanie

MORELAND

BOOKS INC.

Edited by Lisa Hollett, Silently Correcting Your Grammar
Proofreading by Sisters Get Lit.erary
Cover design by Feed Your Dreams Designs

Cover content is for illustrative purposes only and any person depicted on the cover is a model.

fiction, which have been used without permission. The publication/use of these trademarks is not authorized, associated with, or sponsored by the trademark owners.

Readers with concerns about content or subjects depicted can check out the content advisory on my website:
https://melaniemoreland.com/extras/fan-suggestions/content-advisory/

## DEDICATION

*To all who enjoyed the found family,*
*the small town, and the love.*
*Who asked for more.*
*This one is for you.*
*Thanks for being part of the journey.*

*And to my Matthew—who is my found family and*
*love.*
*Always for you.*

# CHAPTER ONE

## Dom

I hit the button, the large garage door rolling down smoothly into place. I engaged the locks then headed to the office, wiping my hands and shifting my shoulders. It had been a busy morning, and I had plans for another active afternoon.

Chase was shutting down the computer, his jacket already on. I laughed at his enthusiasm. "Anxious, kid?"

He grinned at me and shrugged. "I don't want Hannah doing all the painting without me."

I grinned back. The kid had it bad for his supposed "roommate." He was already falling for her, and I had a feeling that wasn't going to change anytime soon.

"I'll stop and get some cold beer and pop."

"That'll be great. Hannah's mom is coming to help. Charly and Gabby. With all those hands, it'll go fast. I know they have food planned too. We can eat before we start working."

"Sounds great."

"Thanks for doing this, Dom."

I waved him off. "Anytime. I'll see you at the house

shortly. I'm gonna grab a shower. I got pretty dirty with that valve job."

"Great. See you soon!"

He left, and I headed to the bathroom at the back, stepping into the shower. The hot water felt good on my shoulders, and I soaped up, my mind drifting as I thought about the direction my life had taken.

Not long ago, I had stopped at the garage, my vehicle giving me trouble as I was taking a drive on a nice day, exploring the countryside. I had been pleased to see Stefano Borrelli, a mechanic I had worked with previously, was in the shop. Between us, we found the problem fast, and as we chatted, he told me they were looking for experienced mechanics to help run the place. One thing led to another, and I met Maxx Reynolds, the owner of the garage. We liked each other, and before I knew it, I had a new job.

I found a small house in Lomand, a slightly larger town than Littleburn, where the garage was located, and I moved in to the furnished space right away. As the weeks went by and I settled, I discovered how much I liked the two little towns. The people. The garage.

They were a close-knit unit here at Reynolds Restorations and had accepted me as one of their own. It was the first time in years I felt the desire to settle in one place for a while. I had a feeling when I was with the group —as if I had found something I had been looking for. They were like a family, something I had longed for but never thought I would be part of. I liked being a member of the crowd, accepted for who I was. No questions, no judgments. They included me in their dinners, the after-work drinks. Family time.

I, in turn, wanted to be part of their projects. Help out where I could. I enjoyed the camaraderie and the time spent with them as a group or one-on-one. Chase and I were close, working together the most. He was a good guy, and he had shared his painful backstory with me. He was like a little brother to all of us, and I liked spending time with him. I also loved playing with all the kids, their innocent laughter bringing back memories that, at times, were painful, yet made me smile.

As I stepped out of the shower, I wondered if perhaps I would reach out again. Try to reconnect to a piece of my past that I longed to be part of my life. I sighed as I towel-dried my hair, already feeling the pull of disappointment. I knew it would probably never happen. Every time I had tried, it had failed. Yet, time and again, I attempted to bridge the large gap, hoping against hope this time it would work.

I studied my face in the mirror, shaking my head. I looked upset. I always did when I thought about the past. The things I regretted. I couldn't think about it now. I had places to be and people waiting for me.

The person who wanted nothing to do with me needed to be dealt with another day.

I would soak up the good today.

The bad was always waiting.

I walked into Chase's place, the sounds of laughter greeting me. I strolled into the kitchen, smiling at Chase, who was talking to two women. One was his new roommate, Hannah. Or Cinnamon, as he called her, referring to the hundreds of freckles scattered on her cheeks and the bridge of her nose. She was a police officer whom he had met on a bad night when he was intoxicated and down. And instead of arresting him, she had reached out to Brett, who had come to help him. Chase crushed on her immediately. She showed up when he was advertising for a roommate, and he was a total goner. It was amusing to watch him navigate his feelings and actions.

But it was the other woman who got my attention. Shorter than Hannah. Curvier. Brick-red hair hung over her shoulder in a thick braid. The loose shirt and tight leggings she wore were simple but incredibly sexy on her lush form. Intelligent, hazel eyes were set under delicate brows, and although her freckles were far fewer in number than Hannah's, they were no less appealing. Our eyes locked and held, and for a moment, the earth stood still around us. She captivated me instantly, and from her frank appraisal, she approved of what she saw. Realizing I was staring, and we had an audience, I shook my head and set down the cans of beer and pop. "I, ah, brought refreshments."

I held out my hand, needing to connect with the woman. "Dom," I said, my voice sounding rough to my ears. I cleared my throat. "Dom Salvatore."

"Hi," the woman murmured. "Cherry Gallagher. I'm Hannah's—"

I cut her off. "Older sister."

"…mother," she finished.

I blew out a whistle. "Impossible."

"I assure you, I am."

"They don't make mothers like you where I come from."

Cherry tossed her hair and blushed. "Then you've lived a sheltered life."

Chase stared between us, a grin on his lips. Hannah looked at us, surprise on her face.

Cherry's teasing made me smile. "I guess I need to expand my horizons." I crossed my arms. "Maybe you could help me with that—" I paused, rubbing my bottom lip and staring at her "—Cherry Gallagher."

She lifted her eyebrows. "I wouldn't hold my breath, Mr. Salvatore."

I liked her defiance. "We'll see about that."

She swept past me, and I caught a whiff of her scent. It was warm and appealing. Much like her. "I'll go tell the girls to come get something to eat."

I spun on my heel and followed her, unable to resist. "I'll make sure she finds them," I told Chase and Hannah over my shoulder.

I heard Chase chuckle, but I ignored him. I was too mesmerized by the way Cherry's hips swayed as she walked in front of me. Her ass was a perfect rounded peach in her leggings, and I had the craziest desire to grab hold of it and bite.

She glanced over her shoulder, one eyebrow raised. "I know my way, Mr. Salvatore."

"Just ensuring your safety, Cherry G."

"Are we expecting surprise mercenary attacks?"

"If we were expecting them, they wouldn't be surprise attacks, would they?"

She began to laugh, tossing her head. Her thick braid fell down her back, almost to her ass. I had the sudden longing to tug it from the elastic that wrapped it up and see how beautiful the cascade of dark red looked. How it felt in my fist.

I faltered in my steps, my cock swelling in my jeans. Jesus, I needed to get a grip. I couldn't grab her and pull her into one of the bedrooms and have my way with her.

Yet.

But I had a feeling Cherry Gallagher and I would be getting close soon enough.

At least, we would if I had anything to say about it.

I was impressed by the spread the two Gallagher women laid out. Sandwiches, dips, veggies. Cheese and crackers. Cut-up fruit. Cupcakes. It all looked delicious, and I piled a plate and casually strolled across the room once Cherry had hers, staying nearby. She eyeballed me then began to eat as if resigned to me being close. I had plans to get much closer, if possible. When they started discussing how to tackle the project, I interjected and offered to do the hall with Cherry. "I'll do the high parts. Cherry here can look after the bottom. Once we're finished, we'll move into the living room since it's the biggest area, and we can help with that," I said with a pleased nod. It was a great plan. The hallway was narrow, so the chances of us brushing up against each other were high. I liked the idea.

Cherry didn't object, although she didn't express any excitement over the idea either. I took it as a win. I watched her as we ate, staying close. Charly and Gabby had arrived, and it took Charly all of two seconds to figure out the attraction I was feeling to Cherry. Charly looked satisfied, as if it had all been her idea. I noticed the amused glances Hannah and Chase were sharing when I would talk to Cherry or add another sandwich to her plate, not wanting her to be hungry. I ignored all of them.

Charly was enthusiastic with her response to my announcement of working with Cherry. "Good plan, Dom. I bet you'll make a great team. Gabby and I will start the living room. We've painted together before." She smiled at Chase. "You and Hannah can tackle your room, okay, Chase?"

"Sure," he agreed easily, no doubt as pleased with the pairing as I was.

"We have the brushes, rollers, and paint trays in each

area all ready to go," Cherry said. "And the right paint. Lots of rags, plus the stepladders."

"So organized," I muttered. "I do love me a woman who is organized."

Cherry snorted. "You have to be. Try being a single mother who has to get her kid ready for school and be at work on time every day. You learn fast."

I lifted one eyebrow, staring at her. I admired her directness, and I had a feeling she had been, and still was, an awesome mother. Her daughter was a lovely woman, and they seemed to be very similar in many ways. I liked how she returned my glances, never backing down, even when a soft flush would color her cheeks.

I really wanted to know if she flushed in other places as well. And I was desperate to know what she was whispering to Hannah. I had no doubt it was about me.

Maxx and Stefano walked in, surprising everyone. They announced we were all invited to dinner after and that Mama Rosa was cooking. I was pleased to be included, recalling Stefano's mother's cooking fondly. Besides, it gave me more time with Cherry.

A double win, in my opinion.

The food disappeared fast, as it always did with this crew, then we got to work. In the hallway, I picked up a paint can and a brush, carrying the small ladder to the spot we agreed to start in.

"I can edge the higher parts," Cherry informed me. "I'm quite capable of climbing a ladder."

I tilted my head, studying her. "I'm well aware you can probably do anything you set your mind to, Cherry G, but why don't you save the climbing for later?"

"Later?"

I leaned down, grinning at her. "You can climb me."

"In your dreams."

I dropped my voice, bending close to her ear. "Oh, you'll be starring in those, Cherry. Trust me."

Her eyes widened, and the flush on her cheeks was deep this time. She tossed her head, her braid swinging side to side. "You are too much."

Unable to resist, I picked up the heavy braid and tucked it over her shoulder. The hair felt soft under my fingers, and I had to tamp down the impulse to lift it to my nose and inhale the soft scent. "Or maybe, I'm just enough."

"We need to start painting," she insisted, looking flustered.

"Okay. Let's go."

Her ass was spectacular when she bent over. I had her start on the other half of the hall, ogling her shamelessly every time she added paint to her brush then stretched down to edge the trim. I was faster, but I purposely slowed down so I could watch her longer. We didn't talk much, but on occasion, one of us would ask a question.

"Are you liking it here?" she asked. "It seems like a nice little town. Safe."

"It's great," I agreed. "Far better pace than Toronto."

"And safe," she repeated.

"Safe, yes," I agreed, sensing she needed that reassurance.

"Chase seems very nice."

"He is. He'll watch over Hannah. We all will."

That earned me a wide smile. I wanted more of those.

"So, her mother," I mused. "Still finding that hard to believe."

"I had her when I was eighteen. I'm forty-six. Entirely possible."

"Two years younger than me."

"Is that relevant? You like women younger?"

I chuckled. She was determined to paint me with the wrong brush. It was amusing. Vexing, but amusing. "No. Two years is perfect."

She abruptly changed the subject, making me grin. "Do you like painting?" she asked.

"It's not my favorite hobby," I admitted.

"Why are you here, then?"

I leaned on the ladder, meeting her eyes. I wanted to be sure she heard me. Understood me.

"Chase is my friend. He's a great kid who's had some bad raps in his life. I care for him a lot. We get along well. He needed help—I'm there for him. He'd do the same for me. Hell, he does it for everyone. It's his time to get shown he means something. So, anything he needs, anything Hannah needs, I'm there." I paused as her eyes widened. "I look after those I care about, Cherry G. There aren't a lot of people I call friends, so those I do get all of me. Painting? I'm in. Moving some furniture? Let me rub on some Voltaren, and I'll be right over. Had too much to drink and need a ride? There in five. Need to talk? The coffee is on. Whatever you need. That's what a friend does."

Something in her face softened.

"That goes for you too."

"You hardly know me."

"But I want to."

She blinked. "Okay, then. Um, I'll remember that."

"Good." I nodded and went back to painting.

At one point, she studied the wall, taking the brush from my hand and climbing the ladder. I held it, curious as to what she was doing. She frowned in concentration as she ran the brush over my work, ensuring the line was straight where I had missed a small area. She teetered a little, and I gripped her thighs, holding her. "Steady," I murmured.

Her muscles contracted under my touch, and I heard her fast inhale of air. Unable to resist, I stroked my thumbs in circles on her leggings, eliciting another tightening of her legs. I met her narrowed eyes. "Making sure you don't fall. Any other missed spots?" I asked innocently.

"Over there, in the corner," she replied as she climbed down.

I moved the ladder, and Cherry edged past me, our bodies sliding against each other. I stifled a groan as I felt her curves sweep by my torso, her full breasts pressing into my chest. I swore I heard her whimper, and she stumbled. I reached out and caught her around the waist, holding her upright.

"Okay there, Cherry G?"

She looked up, and I stared down. Her eyes were mesmerizing, the colors swirling in them making them unique and pretty. She blinked at me, caught in my gaze. We were so close, I could feel her rapid breaths on my skin. Sensed her instinct to move closer, even as she began to pull away. I brushed away a loose tendril from her cheek, wanting to follow the path with my lips. I began to lower my head when she made an odd squeaking noise and stepped away.

"Oops, almost got paint on you. I-I need a break. Going to get some water. Cool down. It's hot, isn't it? All this work?" she babbled.

"It's not the work that's hot."

Her eyes widened, and without another word, she turned and fled.

I let her go, laughing under my breath. It had gotten hotter.

And once again, my jeans had gotten tighter.

Painting had never been this stimulating before. I doubted it ever would be again.

# CHAPTER TWO

## Dom

I watched Cherry the rest of the evening. I sat with Chase, discussing a few other renos he was planning, but my gaze didn't stray from the pretty redhead very often. Our eyes met time and again, and she was always the first to look away. But I saw the color in her cheeks and the way she tossed her hair, as if attempting to dismiss me, only to glance my way once more a few moments later. I liked her looking at me. I hoped she liked what she saw as much as I enjoyed staring at her. More than once, I tamped down the urge to go sit beside her. I wanted her attention, to talk to her, get her number. Maybe steal a kiss or wrap my hand around hers. But I resisted. I had the feeling, despite her bravado, she was skittish, and I didn't want to scare her off.

Later, as I was getting a coffee in the kitchen, she walked in, her hands filled with plates and cutlery. I had noticed how she jumped up to help whenever she could. I found that appealing. She wasn't a woman who expected to be waited on. Although if she asked, I would happily do so.

I reached out, taking the stack from her hands and setting it on the counter. "Coffee?" I asked.

"Please."

I poured her a cup, adding cream and a single sugar cube, handing it to her.

"How did you know?" she queried.

"I was watching earlier. I took notes."

She lifted one eyebrow at me, her lips pursed. "Is that so?"

I nodded, leaning against the counter. "I took a lot of notes."

She tossed her head, and I grinned behind the mug, taking a sip.

"Is that so?" she repeated.

I nodded. "You're highly organized. You like to be in charge. You're not afraid of hard work. You're a great mother, and you extend that maternal instinct to other young people. There is nothing pretentious or fake about you. And when you're feeling anxious or unsure, you toss your hair." I winked at her. "I like that."

She blinked.

"You are incredibly sexy and have no idea how sensuous you are. You have a great ass, and I hope you wear leggings a lot when I see you. I hope I get to discover how that ass feels gripped in my hands one day." I took a sip of coffee. "Soon."

She looked around the kitchen as if making sure I was speaking to her, not someone else.

"Yes, you, Cherry G."

"You can't say things like that to me."

"I think I already did."

"You said you liked me as a friend."

"No, I said I treated my friends well. I'll treat you even better."

"I-I have to put these in the dishwasher," she sputtered, turning away. I saw the color in her cheeks and the way her eyes glittered under the light. She liked what I was saying.

I tilted my head, grinning widely. She was methodical as she slid the plates into the rack—not unexpected. But it was the fact that she bent as she did so, thrusting that perfect ass in my direction again. I drained my coffee and approached her. I put my mug in the dishwasher, my fingers brushing her hand. She stilled, looking up. I was close to her again, inhaling her fragrance, feeling her warmth. Our eyes locked, the heat between us sizzling. When she unconsciously licked her lips, I groaned quietly. "Very soon, I'm going to kiss those lips," I murmured.

She looked dazed. "But not now?" she whispered.

"No. If I start, I won't stop, and your daughter and her friends will get quite the show," I replied, wrapping my hand around her thick braid. "But soon." I tugged gently, tipping her head back. I pressed a kiss to her forehead. "Until then, Cherry G."

I turned and walked away before I did something I shouldn't. I heard her hard exhale of air as I walked toward the door.

"Don't count on it, Mr. Salvatore."

I grinned as I walked out the door.

*There she was.*

Chase was quiet that week. He'd been so excited and upbeat before the painting party, and I wondered what had happened. I didn't like to pry, and I was grateful when I saw him talking to Charly privately. I knew how close they were and that she would help him solve whatever was bothering him. At least, I hoped she did. I wasn't so good with conversations involving other people's feelings. Although, if a friend needed me to listen, I would try. I could barely understand my own emotions, never mind anyone else's. None of the guys in the garage were good at discussing feelings with each other. Charly excelled at it— whether you wanted to share or not. Somehow, she dragged it out of you.

Chase and I had plans this weekend after we shut the garage. We were heading into Toronto to a large building supply store. They had a bigger selection of materials at better prices than we could get in the tiny hardware store in Littleburn. Then I was taking him to my favorite barbecue place so we could stuff ourselves with the best barbecue around. And I planned on picking his brain about Cherry. Any little piece of information I could get would be helpful. I was especially hoping for her number or even her place of employment so I could go and find her.

She was on my mind constantly. Her pretty eyes and unique hair color were intriguing. The way she took charge and treated the people around her was as endearing as it was a turn-on. And that ass. Spectacular. So was her attitude. She wouldn't suffer fools easily, and I had a feeling she was going to be a challenge.

One I would enjoy.

I only had to make her realize she would as well.

That right there was the first hurdle to overcome.

But I was ready.

## CHERRY

I finished up the client, spritzing on some hair spray and tucking an errant curl into place. Handing her the mirror to allow her to inspect my work, I was pleased when she smiled. "Awesome as usual, Cherry."

After chatting with her for a moment, I began to clean up my station. She was the last client of the day. My daughter, Hannah, had called to say she was coming in early. We were going for supper and would spend the evening watching a movie and catching up. Tomorrow was a big shopping day for us. She needed linens and house stuff for her new place, and I loved to shop the warehouse sales with her. You never knew what you might find.

I waved goodbye to the other stylists and headed up the back steps to my apartment over the salon. Inside, I grabbed a quick shower to rid myself of the chemical smell since I had done a couple of perms today, and that always left an odor. After making a cup of coffee and curling up on the sofa with a sigh, I shut my eyes, feeling tired. I was always tired by the end of the week. Standing all day and the constant strain on my shoulders and arms as I cut hair took a toll. My back ached lately, and I had to admit, I wasn't sure how much longer I wanted to cut hair. It had been great when I was younger. I owned my own place and could make my hours around Hannah's schedule. Standing all day didn't bother my much-younger body the way it did now.

When I'd closed my shop and gone to work for someone else, I had been glad to be rid of the constant headaches of owning my own business. The staff, the worry over bills, maintenance, supplies, and troublesome clients were now someone else's concern. I found this job and the small apartment right over the shop, and it had worked out fine, although the apartment wasn't a place I saw myself in forever. Hannah was on her own, and I didn't need the house anymore. It had felt good to leave it. Leave the memories that, even after all these years, stayed with me in that house. I could never open the door without remembering the day I'd found Mike's commanding officer on the other side with the news that had changed my life—our lives—forever.

I sighed, pushing away those dark thoughts. I had found the strength to keep going, and I built a nice life for Hannah and me. With her moving to Lomand, I missed her a lot. We were very close. I was looking forward to seeing her. Having her catch me up on the news.

The image of a tall, sexy man came to mind, and I wondered if she would have any information on him.

Dom Salvatore.

I shook my head to clear it.

He was a force of nature. Cocky. Sure of himself. Outspoken and direct.

And so incredibly out of bounds.

I was struck by his masculine beauty the moment he walked into the kitchen. His tattooed biceps bulged, carrying three cases of pop and beer. His T-shirt hugged his torso, his long legs encased in jeans. He was muscular and fit. Tall and broad across his shoulders. Lean at the waist.

He sported scruff on his face, the dark shadow highlighting his ruggedness. His brown hair was short, and his dark eyes smoldered. I couldn't stop looking at him.

And he stared back. All day. Every time I looked, he was locked on me. And when he spoke, his voice made the hairs on my neck stand up. I felt something I hadn't experienced in years. Pure, unadulterated desire.

And he scared me.

I sighed, wrapping my hand around my mug. He'd been on my mind all week. His low laughter. His sultry looks in my direction. The way he teased me. Found excuses to be close. To touch me. I thought of the seriousness on his face when he answered my question about painting. He was all swagger and teasing, but below the surface, I had begun to have the feeling there was more than met the eye. He simply didn't show it to many people.

I swore I still felt the press of his mouth on my forehead. That sweet, intimate gesture stayed with me more than any caress a man had bestowed on me in years.

Not that there had been many. After my husband died, I had been too busy trying to stay in one piece and raise Hannah to have time to date. I'd had a low period a couple of years after I lost Mike when I'd allowed myself to try. It had ended in disaster, and I swore never again. Losing Mike had almost ended me, and what had happened when I'd trusted the wrong man had taken me a long time to recover from. I concentrated on Hannah, making her the focal point.

As she'd grown up and needed less of my time, I'd found I wasn't really interested in having a man come around and try to change my life. I liked being independent. Not having to ask for permission to do anything. There were times I was lonely and longed for a man's touch, another person to share my life with, but I quickly got over those moments, remembering what had happened when I'd tried. I dated a few times, although single mothers were not really sought-after. Most of the men I went for a first date with never called for a second. The few who did seemed to resent the fact that Hannah would take priority, so being alone was the way life went.

But now, Hannah was grown with a life of her own.

And I was lonely at times.

A fact I had a feeling Dom Salvatore would be happy to rectify.

However briefly.

The question was, would I be happy with a fast, passionate affair? A man like him, a reformed bad boy, was probably only interested in a short-term thing.

Was I?

Another thought struck me. What if he wasn't what I thought he was? What if his interest was real and genuine? What if the man was exactly what he claimed to be?

Was I prepared for that?

I groaned. Neither scenario helped. I was still confused and nervous.

And I hated that.

Hannah arrived as I finished my coffee, the caffeine giving me the needed pep. I hadn't been sleeping as well lately, the image of dark, smoldering eyes and strong hands waking me often.

Not that I would tell my daughter that.

We went to our favorite pho place and chatted. She showed me pictures of how she was putting together the rooms we'd helped to paint.

"Looks great, jellybean," I said. I was surprised how much Chase was allowing her to do, but I sensed he wanted her to feel at home with him—on every level. I had to admit, I liked him a great deal, and I hoped Hannah did as well.

I paused at a picture. "What is this?"

"Oh." Hannah wiped her mouth. "Chase bought a new bed. He never thought to buy sheets, so I'm going to pick him up a set."

"He's a nice boy."

She smirked. "He is hardly a boy, Mom. He is a couple years older than me."

I waved my hand. "Everyone is a boy or girl to me these days, Hannah. I'm far too old."

She laughed, shaking her head. "Please. Did you see the shock on everyone's faces when I introduced you as my mom? They all thought you were a sister or a friend." She dipped her spring roll in the spicy mixture of soy and sriracha. "And Dom was certainly transfixed."

I rolled my eyes, feigning disinterest at her words. "Bossy, that one. Far too forward."

Hannah grinned.

"And we're not here to talk about him." I picked up my teacup, sipping it. "What is going on with you and Chase?"

"He's my landlord. And roomie. We're friends—I think."

I shook my head. "Hannah, baby. I'm your mom. I could see the sparks between you from across the room. You light up like a Christmas tree when he's around. And he zeroes in on you the second he walks into the room."

She sighed. "I thought there was something, but since we painted, he's been…I don't know…*off*. We even argued. He apologized, but he is upset about something. I feel like I've hurt him somehow, and I don't know how to fix it. He's polite and accommodating, but distant."

"Do you think the whole painting his house was too much? All the people invading his space?"

"I don't know. Except he adores Charly and Gabby. He's very close with the guys, and they help one another a lot. The only new faces were us. I think maybe he's rethinking having a female roommate." She laughed without humor. "Me, specifically."

"Has he said that?"

"No. In fact, last night, he looked upset when he wondered if I was questioning the whole thing. He told me he liked me there. He practically begged me not to move out."

I finished my soup, then pushed away my bowl. "Maybe he has stronger feelings for you and isn't sure how to express them. You two looked pretty cozy on the weekend."

"Well, now we're two icebergs crossing in the ocean. Close but not touching."

"What is he doing this weekend?"

"Spending the afternoon tomorrow supply shopping, then he and Dom are going to some bar Dom likes an hour away."

I snorted. "No doubt a great stomping ground for pickups. Not too close to home that you have to worry about a relationship developing."

She grimaced, and I patted her hand. "Sorry, jellybean. I was thinking more of Dom than Chase. He has that love-'em-and-leave-'em vibe. The whole bad-boy thing. Except he's a little past that." I shook my head. "I'm just not sure he knows it."

Hannah shrugged. "I've talked to him a couple of times. He seems genuine. Maybe his 'vibe' is something you're putting on him."

"Why would I do that?"

"Because you liked him, and it makes you nervous."

I tossed my hair defiantly. "No, I didn't."

"He is pretty sexy with that intense look and the tattoos and all. Lots of swagger."

"Takes more to turn my head than some swagger, daughter of mine." I paused. "Although his, ah, *swagger* is pretty nice. Especially from the back view."

We both started to laugh, and it felt good to make light

of the situation. I didn't want to think of him any other way, even if he was different from the first impression I had of him. I wasn't looking for a relationship.

We talked more about Chase, their budding relationship, and her future plans. I got the sense Chase was going to be a huge part of them. I felt pleased, knowing she might have found someone. I liked the fact that she was living in a smaller town. It was safer in so many ways. I had hated the fact that she'd decided to be a cop like her father, but I had chosen to support her rather than drive her away. When she'd been hurt in the line of duty, I was grateful she'd decided to take a job in a smaller place. Lomand and the surrounding area were very low on the crime scale, and even though it meant I didn't see her as often, it was a good compromise. She was safe. That was the most important thing. She was the most important thing in my life.

And although I missed her being close, the fact that she was more sheltered and happier was far more important.

# CHAPTER THREE

## Dom

I walked into the small diner in Lomand and sat on one of the barstools. The place was busy, but my favorite waitress, Donna, came over, pouring me a cup of coffee. "The usual?" she asked.

"Please."

I sipped my coffee, contemplating what to do with my day off. I had no errands to run today or things to be handled. I was only taking the day because Maxx insisted. I'd prefer to be at the garage, but I was informed I had to take my time away. Although Chase and I had picked out his building materials, we were in a holding pattern until the supplies came in. He'd been in a far better mood the past while, and I assumed it had a lot to do with his progressing relationship with Hannah. Chase didn't say much, but his smiles and demeanor said it all for him.

I was happy for the kid. He deserved it.

I was brought out of my musings by a voice murmuring my name. I glanced up, surprised to see Hannah Gallagher. Chase's girl. She was dressed in her uniform, her bright-red hair pulled back from her face, but she was smiling.

"Hannah," I greeted her, standing and dropping a kiss to her cheek. "How is my favorite officer this morning?"

She laughed. "Good, Dom. You?"

"Never better."

Donna slid my bagel on the counter. "Morning, Hannah. Coffee?"

I grabbed the chance. "Sit with me for a few minutes."

Hannah looked pleased. "Sure. I'm on my break. Coffee and a bagel too, Donna."

"Coming right up."

We moved to a booth, and she slid in across from me. "Not working today?"

I chuckled, shaking my head. "Maxx is making me take a day off."

She sipped her coffee. "Chase says you're the hardest worker he knows."

I lifted a shoulder. "I like to stay busy. Still finding my place here, so being at the garage fills the time."

Donna appeared with Hannah's bagel, and we added cream cheese and ate for a moment.

"How, ah, is your mom?" I asked.

Hannah grinned. "Good. Busy at the salon. I spoke with her last night."

"She must miss you."

"Yes. I miss her too."

I cleared my throat. "She's not seeing anyone?" I let the question hang in the air.

"No." Hannah bit into her bagel, chewing as she regarded me thoughtfully. "She doesn't date much."

"A beautiful woman like her should."

She grinned again. "You think my mom is beautiful?"

"Absolutely." I paused. "In fact, I'd like to take her out, Hannah. Would you be okay with that?"

"Not my decision, but I'd have no problem with it," she responded. "Mom is really independent, Dom. Stubborn."

"I figured that much. I liked that about her."

"She's never been into casual relationships."

I met her gaze, seeing the questions in her eyes.

"Neither am I."

"You live an hour away."

"So did Rosa and Mack. They made it work."

She studied me as she finished her bagel, wiping her fingers. "She is…" She trailed off, looking for the right word.

"Skittish," I finished for her. I had a feeling there was a story there, but I wasn't going to ask Hannah. I wanted to hear it from Cherry.

"Yes." She paused. "She thinks you're a love-them-and-leave-them type."

I chuckled. "In my youth, maybe—a long time ago. People change. I want to get to know her."

"To what end?" she asked.

"That will be a decision for the two of us." I took a sip of coffee. "If I can convince her to go on a date first." I lifted my eyebrows. "But I need to get her number."

Hannah finished her breakfast, wiping her mouth. She stood, placing her hat back on her head. "Mom works at the Right Angle on Kingston. She takes walk-ins." She eyed me with a grin. "You look a little scruffy, Dom. Maybe a trim would help. You have the day off after all."

Then with a grin, she bent and kissed my cheek. "She might give you her number herself."

I watched her leave with a smile, finishing my coffee.

My day suddenly had a purpose.

And its name was Cherry Gallagher.

## CHERRY

I was folding towels when I heard the giggles. I rolled my eyes, picking up another towel. I was getting too old for this. The staff got younger and younger. I felt more ancient every day. It was a lovely little salon, and I had a steady clientele I had brought with me from my old place. The owner had her regulars, but the new staff was building their own customer bases.

The salon was steady for a Wednesday. Not crazy, but okay. There had been a few walk-ins, and the girls had been eyeing up some of the younger clients. Listening to their comments at times made me wish I had earplugs.

"Oh my gawd…" Janey stage-whispered as they came to the back. "So haaaawt for an old guy."

"I'd do him," Lana responded. "He could be my daddy anytime."

"Girls," I hissed. "Stop it."

They looked at me, not caring. "You have a walk-in. I put him at your station," Lana said.

I frowned. "I'm not taking walk-ins today. They're for you girls."

"He asked for you." She leaned close. "He is so intense."

Janey fanned herself. "Those eyes. So dark and dreamy."

I frowned, a small tremor starting in my stomach. I hadn't given my card out lately. Why would a walk-in ask for me directly?

Unless it was someone I knew.

Intense. Dark eyes.

It couldn't be.

I fluffed my hair and peeked in the mirror to make sure my apron was on properly and I had no lipstick on my teeth. I straightened my shoulders and headed out front.

I met those dark, intense eyes in the mirror as I approached. The way he watched me sent shivers down my spine. It was as if I was the only person in the room. The world.

"Mr. Salvatore."

He grinned, his white teeth flashing in amusement. "Cherry G."

"What are you doing here?"

He ran a hand through his hair. "I was informed I was scruffy. I thought you could help with that."

I stood behind him, meeting his eyes in the mirror. "Are there no barbers in Lomand?"

"Not pretty ones like you." His gaze became heated. "I want *your* hands on me, Cherry. Not a stranger's."

A thrill ran through me at his words. The truth was I had wanted to touch his hair the moment I met him. Run my fingers through his thick locks and see if they were as soft as they looked. I wanted to touch him.

"And your scruff?" I asked, hating how thick my voice sounded.

He ran a hand along his chin. "Do what you want with me," he said quietly. "I'm yours."

The tremor in my stomach became a full-blown earthquake at his words. I had to fist my hands at my sides to stop the tremble in them. I swallowed hard, squaring my shoulders. "Well, let's get you shampooed, then."

He followed me to the sinks. I waved off the girls, both of them eager to be the one to wash his hair.

I wasn't sharing. Not today.

I got him settled, trying to ignore the way he stared at me. It was constant, his eyes never leaving me. I could feel the heat of them with every movement. I had to shut my eyes and draw in a deep breath, trying to find my equilibrium. I had a feeling, with Dom Salvatore, that was going to be hard to come by.

Washing his hair was an intimate experience—something I didn't expect. As I leaned over him, his scent drifted up through the heat of the water. Masculine. Heady. He sighed as I began to shampoo his hair, the strands as soft as I'd thought they would be under my fingers. His eyes fluttered shut as I massaged his scalp, a small groan of pleasure escaping from his mouth. As I leaned over to grab a comb, my breasts pressed into his face, and I swore we both whimpered. My nipples felt tight and hard under the layers of my clothing, yet I swore I felt his heat burn right through the fabric. Being this close to him, I felt the ache between my thighs. One I had long forgotten about. I had to fight off the urge to climb onto his lap and kiss the hell out of him.

The girls would have a field day with that visual.

Finally, I finished, wrapping his head in a towel and stepping back. "You can sit up now. Follow me."

He blew out a long breath, opening his eyes, the stark desire and passion in them taking my breath away. "I'll follow you anywhere, woman."

Flustered, I glanced away, my gaze falling on his lap. I wasn't the only one affected. His thick jeans held a bulge that both promised and threatened. It was all I could do not to groan at the sight of it. Instead, I averted my eyes. "This way," I said briskly.

He chuckled as he followed. No doubt my cheeks were on fire and he knew exactly what I had seen.

I draped a cape over him. Normally, I would chat with a client. Especially new ones. Draw them out and establish a rapport, hoping to gain a repeat customer. With Dom, my words had dried up. It was all I could do to concentrate on his hair, trimming his scruff. Aside from a few murmured questions and responses, we were silent.

But the tension between us was palpable. He watched me. Every move. Every time I looked up, his eyes were on me. I saw the way his hands clutched at the arms of the chair as if he was stopping himself from touching me.

And I ached for him to do so.

But I tamped everything down. Snipped and combed. Shaped and cut. I used my clippers on his scruff, trying not to show any reaction as I touched his face. His skin. I jumped a little as he gripped my hip. "Keeping you steady," he said.

His touch only made the flame inside me burn brighter. I felt it everywhere.

I blew his hair dry, using the lowest setting, enjoying the feel of his hair. That was the only time he shut his eyes, and I knew he was enjoying it. His shoulders relaxed, and a smile played on his full mouth.

I wanted to kiss that mouth.

I stepped back, shutting off the dryer and giving his hair a final comb-through. "All done."

He opened his eyes, and I held up a mirror so he could see the back. "Looks great," he praised. "Best haircut I've ever had."

I tried not to laugh at his low muttering that followed. "Most stimulating as well."

He followed me to the front, and I gave him the total. He dug into his pocket, handing me too much money. I shook my head, and he frowned.

"Your tip. For excellent work." Before I could protest, he smiled. "Now I'll take you to lunch."

"Um, no. I have another client coming in."

He shook his head. "According to the screen behind you, you're free for another hour. Lunch, Cherry G. I'm going to feed you."

"No, I, ah, I have other things I have to do."

The salon owner came over, looking between us. "Problem?" she asked.

Dom smiled at her. Charming. Friendly. "I want to take my girl here to lunch, but she seems to think she can't leave."

*His girl?* I opened my mouth to protest, but Connie cut me off, looking at me as if I were crazy. "Go to lunch with your man, Cherry. The girls can finish the towels." She held out her hand. "I'm Connie."

Dom smiled again, lifting her hand to his mouth and kissing it. "Thanks, Connie. Pleasure to meet you. I'll have her back in time for her next client. I hardly get to see her, so any time I can grab is awesome."

Connie blushed. Actually blushed. "Oh, take your time. Mrs. Jenkins likes a cup of coffee before her appointment. I'll chat with her, and Janey can wash her hair. That'll give you two lovebirds some extra time." She nudged me. "You can fill me in later." She winked and walked away before I could inform her I wasn't his girl or a lovebird. I turned to Dom, glaring.

He grinned. "Come on, Cherry G." He wiped his bottom lip. "I'm starving."

"I'll get my purse," I muttered through tight lips as I tugged my apron over my head.

"No need. Lunch is on me." He held out his hand. "Let's go."

I felt every eye on me. Inquisitiveness was rife in the air, and I knew I'd be bombarded with questions when I got back.

"Fine."

And despite being annoyed with him, I couldn't dismiss the fact that my hand felt right wrapped up in his.

Which only made me angrier.

# CHAPTER FOUR

## Dom

She was pissed off. The color in her cheeks was high, and her shoulders were set back. But she let me take her hand and lead her across the street to the small restaurant I had noticed. We sat at a booth facing the street. When she had pulled off her apron, her hair had come loose from the ponytail it had been in and now hung in thick waves down her back. The sun caught the dark red, turning it rust and gold. I wanted to wrap it around my hand as I kissed her. Feel it splayed across my chest as she slept on me after I fucked her.

I shook my head to clear it. After a quick perusal of the menu, I ordered a roast beef sandwich and onion rings. Cherry got ham and cheese with a side of coleslaw. We both ordered coffee and water.

I told her about running into Hannah that morning, and we chatted about her and Chase and their new living arrangements. She asked about where I had lived in Toronto. I queried her about the salon. She waited until the food had arrived and we had eaten most of it before she brought up the elephant at the table with us.

"I am not your girl, Mr. Salvatore. I am too old to be anyone's *girl*."

I grinned at her indignant tone. "You prefer to be called my woman?"

"I prefer nothing of the sort. We barely know each other."

"I want to change that."

She looked truly flummoxed. "Why?"

I wiped my mouth and took a sip of coffee, deciding to be blunt. "You cannot deny the attraction between us, Cherry G."

"Infatuation. It will pass."

"I don't think so. I want to explore it with you."

"I'm not looking for a man."

"I wasn't looking for anyone either. But I found you."

She opened her mouth, but nothing came out. She finished her sandwich, pushing her plate away.

"You are very high-handed."

"Determined."

"Bold."

"Confident," I countered.

"Too old to be a playboy."

I threw my head back in laughter. "On that, we agree. I'm not a playboy. The last woman I dated was over a year ago, and she broke it off, not me. She traded me in for a much younger, richer model."

"You live in Lomand."

"I own a car. And a motorcycle. I'm free to come and go anytime. As are you."

"It would be complicated."

"Some of the best things in life are."

She shook her head. "I'm not looking for a relationship."

I studied her. "I know you lost your husband early in life, but something else happened, didn't it?"

She swallowed, suddenly nervous.

"Who hurt you?" I asked.

"It doesn't matter."

"It does to me. I'm not them. I have no desire to hurt you. I want to know you."

"I don't know if I can—I mean, if I want to. Have a relationship, I mean," she repeated, as if making sure I understood her.

I met her eyes. "So you want to just fuck?"

She blinked, startled. "No!"

I nodded, satisfied. "Then we can date." I sat back with a grin. "Fuck, too. I can hardly wait to taste those lips of yours. Both sets."

Once again, she opened her mouth, nothing coming from it. She shook her head as if to clear it.

"You are rude."

"Truthful." I leaned forward, all trace of teasing gone. "I think you're the sexiest woman I have ever seen, Cherry Gallagher. I want you. I have from the moment I saw you. If the salon hadn't had other people in it this morning, I would have dragged you onto my lap and taken you right there." I sat back, our eyes still locked. "And you would have let me. You want me too."

"You're pretty damn sure of yourself." She protested, but her breathing was rapid. Her pupils wide. She clutched the table as if to stop from launching herself at me.

"I know what I see."

She stood. "Well, this time, Mr. Salvatore, you're wrong. Thank you for lunch."

Then she turned and ran. Literally ran away from me. I watched her rush across the street, dodging traffic. She didn't look back, but I knew she felt me watching her.

I let her go. I had seen her number listed on the employee sheet by the cash register. I had memorized it and planned to use it. I had to grin at myself. I was acting out of character, but something about this woman made me irrational. I wanted her. I wanted to get to know her. I wanted her to know me. The real me—not the one she made up in her mind to protect herself.

I turned and headed for my car. I would see her again soon.

If not, I would come back. Cherry G was going to be a challenge.

One I was going to enjoy.

I sent her a text that night.

ME

Hey, Cherry G—it's Dom.

The sunset reminds me of your hair. What is your favorite time of day?

CHERRY

How did you get my number?

ME

The employee list by the cash register.

CHERRY

That was private.

ME

Then it shouldn't have been out where I could see it. I love evenings. Mornings are great too, but I enjoy the quiet of the evening the best. You?

CHERRY

Usually. Unless I'm being bombarded with
messages.

I began to laugh. I loved her spunk.

ME

I'll leave you to your peace. We both like
evenings. Another thing we have in
common. Sweet dreams, Cherry G.

The next day at lunch, I sent another message.

ME

Green is my favorite color. What's yours?

Her reply made me laugh.

CHERRY

Lose my number.

ME

Unusual name for a color. Is that on the
yellow spectrum? I would have thought
blue was more you. Or maybe green
like me.

CHERRY

Silence is golden.

ME

Ah, so it is yellow, then. I can see that—
your smile lights up a room.

CHERRY

Stop it.

ME

But I'm just getting started. What's your
favorite ice cream? Mine is Cherry.

CHERRY

Ha-ha.

ME

Come on. How can we get to know each other if you won't answer?

CHERRY

Mango. I love mango ice cream.

ME

Thank you.

Later that night, I sent another.

ME

Kindle or paperback?

CHERRY

You read?

ME

Very well, actually. I learned in school. I was smart that way. I like holding a book in my hand. You?

It was a while before she responded.

CHERRY

Kindle. I don't have room to store books, so I use the e-reader. I'd love a small room to hold books, though.

ME

I'll keep that in mind.

CHERRY

For?

ME

That's two questions you've asked me,
Cherry G. I knew you liked this idea. And
that is for me to know and you to find out. I
look forward to you finding out a lot
about me.

And liking it.

CHERRY

Good night, Dom.

ME

Sleep well, sweet Cherry.

I grinned as I set down my phone. My plan was working.

I spotted Hannah in the garage the following week. She waved as she left, and I found Chase in the office, eating a burger she had brought him. When I explained I needed a part to finish a job, he offered to drive and pick it up. He was sure Charly would cover and assured me he would work on Saturday to make sure the office was up-to-date.

"Hannah and Cherry are doing a craft fair on Saturday. I can come in and help catch up."

I lifted my eyebrows, a smile playing on my mouth at the welcome news. My challenging woman was proving elusive. I kept texting her, waiting for her to answer, hoping she would initiate a conversation. So far, that hadn't worked, but she did respond to me. I counted that as progress. Last night, we had discussed pets. She loved cats. I liked dogs. When I informed her getting them together as babies would help forge a friendship, I had been met with radio silence. But I knew it got her thinking.

"Cherry's coming for a visit?"

He grinned. "We're going to Zeke's to listen to the band Saturday."

"Isn't that interesting. I was planning on going myself."

"Oh? You like the Broken Owls, do you?"

"One of my favorites."

"Too bad it's the Frozen Tundra playing, then."

I threw back my head in laughter. "You got me. I don't give a care who is playing. It's who will be listening with me that I'm interested in."

Chase laughed with me. "I never had this conversation with you."

"Nope."

"I'll go talk to Charly as soon as I finish my burger."

"I owe you."

He chuckled. "Yep."

I headed back to the garage and the engine rebuild I was working on.

Cherry was coming to town.

How awesome.

I spotted her the moment I walked into the bar. She sat beside Hannah, two fiery redheads, so similar, yet so different. Hannah's hair glowed like a flame, bright and coppery. Cherry's hair was a rich, decadent, aged-whiskey red. Darker, more auburn than the bright of her daughter's.

Sexy as hell hanging past her shoulders, the loose waves shimmering in the light. I should be ashamed of the way I'd spoken to her the other day. The crude words I'd used. But I had wanted to shock her. See her reaction. She hadn't disappointed. I had seen her desire, even as she tried to hide it.

Until she rushed away.

The texts were helping. I threw out all sorts of silly tidbits. Colors, foods, the kind of jeans I liked. Anything to engage. To let her see me.

I ordered a beer and took a sip, scanning the crowd. Mostly younger, but a few people my age. I nodded and greeted some familiar faces, then focused my attention where Cherry sat. I caught Chase's eye, and he grinned, knowing what I was doing. Cherry glanced my way and froze, her shoulders going back and a dull flush settling under the skin of her cheeks. I bit back my smile and approached the table. Chase greeted me as I stopped, and I nodded in acknowledgment.

"Chase. Hannah." I paused, focusing my attention on Cherry. "And Cherry Gallagher. What a pleasure to see you again."

Hannah grinned at me. "Here to listen to some music, Dom?"

"I saw the flyers earlier this week when I was here."

"Hang around the bar a lot, do you?" Cherry asked, her voice cool.

Without waiting for an invitation, I pulled out the chair next to her and swung it around, straddling it. I sat beside her, angling my body her way. I set my beer down on the table and spoke.

"They have great food here. I was having dinner after looking at a couple of houses."

"Oh," she murmured.

"Enjoying your visit?"

"Yes."

I leaned closer. "I hope you enjoy it as much as I enjoyed seeing you last week, Cherry G."

She picked up her drink, taking a sip, ignoring me. I laughed under my breath, relishing the fact that I made her nervous.

The band stepped onstage, and Chase and Hannah got up to dance. I saw the glimmer of sadness in Cherry's eyes as she watched her daughter, even as she smiled. Her hand fidgeted on her lap, a sign of her tension.

"They're good together," she murmured.

"Yes. They're good for each other."

"I hope he doesn't break her heart."

I lifted her hand to my lips, kissing the knuckles. "I think she is the one with the power to destroy him," I observed. "Like her mother."

Cherry's eyes widened and she pulled her hand away, but I caught sight of her smile.

I stood, holding my palm out to her. "Dance with me."

"I don't—I mean, I haven't in a long time."

I grinned. "I bet we move together really well, Cherry G. Trust me." I waggled my fingers.

She rolled her eyes but stood, letting me lead her to the floor. It was crowded, and we were forced to dance closely, which was fine with me. I could feel her body moving easily to the rhythmic beat. When the music slowed, I was happy to pull her into my arms and simply sway with her. I liked how she felt in my embrace. Small. Warm. Matching my steps perfectly. As if she was meant to be there.

I felt the way her breathing picked up as I tugged her closer. Smiled when she slid her hands up my arms, wrapping them around my neck. She sighed as she rested her head on my chest, and unable to resist, I trailed my hand up and down her spine, letting her silky hair brush across my skin.

We danced until the band took a break. Then we sat with Chase and Hannah, enjoying a cold drink. Our eyes kept locking, her inhibitions beginning to fade away as she sipped and relaxed. When I slid my hand over her thigh under the table, she startled, then laid her smaller one on top of mine, squeezing gently.

Conversation was easy between the four of us. It was plain to see how close the two women were. How similar. Chase stared at Hannah with utter adoration on his face. She peeked at him with the same loving expression. Cherry watched them, once again torn between delight over her daughter's happiness and feeling a little sad. I doubted anyone else could see that. She covered it far too well.

But I saw it.

Hannah and Chase got up to dance again, and I leaned close. "Stop worrying, Mom." I tucked a long lock behind her ear, slowly running my fingers over her lobe. "They're good. They're going to be fine."

"Easy for you to say. You didn't raise her."

I felt the flicker of my own pain at her words, but I tamped it down. "You did an amazing job. I think they are lucky they found each other. Relationships are hard, but they're determined."

She pursed her lips. "You're an expert on relationships, Mr. Salvatore? Had a few of them yourself?"

I laughed, knowing she was trying to push my buttons. "I've had my share."

"Hmm." She moved away a little.

I pulled her chair closer, speaking directly into her ear so she could hear me over the music. "I'd like to be in one now. With you," I added, pressing a soft kiss to her lobe.

"I'm not into one-night stands, thank you."

"It doesn't have to be one night, Cherry. I'm not the player you want to think I am."

"Why would I want to think that?"

"So you can justify pushing me away, when we both know you want something totally different."

"And what is it you think I want, Mr. Salvatore?"

"Exactly what I want. To take you to my bed and make you scream my name. My first name. Repeatedly."

She jumped back, shocked. Or turned on. I couldn't tell. Her breathing was rapid and her color high. She stood and hurried away, heading for the ladies' room. I finished my beer, then stood and followed. We weren't finished with this conversation.

## CHERRY

I stared at my reflection in the mirror. My cheeks were flushed. Then I shook my head. Never mind my cheeks. The pink trailed all the way down my neck to my chest. Where my heart was pumping rapidly. From annoyance.

Or something else.

The moment I'd spotted him in the bar, I tensed. Dom Salvatore had been on my mind since the day I had run from him in the restaurant. His showing up at the salon had been enough of a jolt to knock me off my feet. Cutting his hair had been the single most intimate act I'd been part of since my husband had died. Simply touching Dom was akin to an electric shock. Doing so repeatedly had thrown my entire nervous system into overdrive.

Then his coarse words at lunch. His brazenness had taken me back. Stunned me.

Delighted me in ways I never expected.

His utterly dirty words had lit a fire in me I couldn't put out, no matter how hard I tried.

He starred in my dreams. My wet, lurid dreams. I woke

up most mornings, my hand between my legs, wet and aching. Unsatisfied.

His low, raspy voice played over and again in my head.

And then there were his texts. Short little glimpses into him. Teasing, sweet, patient. Endlessly patient, even when I refused to answer. I found myself checking my phone more, hoping one of his comments or queries would be waiting for me.

And then tonight, he was here.

Looking sexy, tall, and intense in his leather jacket, his scruff thick, his eyes locked on me.

Dancing with him was like foreplay. I couldn't recall ever feeling this way toward a man. Even Hannah's dad. We were young, inexperienced, in love. Mike had been a tender lover, sweet in his passion.

The complete opposite of the way Dom Salvatore would be in bed.

I realized I was standing, zoning out in a public restroom, and others were waiting for their turn. I dried my hands, trying to decide what to do. Walk out and leave? Take Dom up on his invite and let him bed me for a night?

I shook my head. I couldn't do that. I was responsible. Hannah was here. What sort of example would that set?

I ignored the laughing voice telling me Hannah was a grown woman and she was out there in the arms of her lover.

*Lover.*

The word alone gave me the shivers.

I tossed my hair, thinking.

Dom was sex incarnate. His penetrating looks and swagger drew attention. I saw how other women stared at him. The younger ones with daddy fantasies on their mind. Older women wondering how it would feel to have him pick them for a night.

Well, I wasn't one of them. I hadn't needed a man for years, and that wasn't changing now. I was a mature woman, and I could handle a little overblown lust. I'd finish my drink and leave Hannah and Chase to enjoy their evening. Dom could find another woman.

I tamped down the jealousy that flooded my chest at the thought of him walking out the door with someone else clutching his firm bicep.

I refused to believe I could feel that way.

Hannah came in, and I waved as she hurried to an empty stall. "Chase is getting fresh drinks," she called.

"Great."

Taking a deep breath, I squared my shoulders. That was settled. One more drink and I was out of there.

Except, Dom was waiting, leaning against the wall at the far end, his arms crossed. He looked intense. Focused. Determined. Sexy.

I swallowed heavily. Really sexy.

*Dammit.*

Somehow, his looking like that made me angry. I needed him remote. Uncaring. Not staring at me like he was starving and I was grade A meat he wanted to devour.

I marched toward him, poking him in the chest. It was like thumping a brick. "Listen, Salvatore. I'm not interested."

"No?" he drawled.

"No. Go away. Stop following me."

"Maybe I'm not waiting for you."

My anger turned to rage so bright, I felt the red of it tinge my eyesight.

"That was fast, wasn't it?"

"But it's what you expect, isn't it, Cherry Gallagher? That you'll say no, and I'll move on and pick someone else." He leaned down, his voice a rumble in my ear I felt all the way through my body. "Here's the deal, though. I don't want anyone else. You're all I think about. Fantasize about. Constantly."

He eased back, tucking a piece of hair behind my ear. "I don't know who hurt you, but I'm not them. I'm not a player, pretty lady. And if you say no, I'll respect that. But I think you want me as much as I want you." He tilted his head. "But you're used to putting yourself second. Denying yourself. Only, this time, you don't have to."

"I-I can't."

He smiled sadly. "Can't or won't?" He shrugged. "I suppose it doesn't matter." In a tender move I didn't expect, he bent and brushed his lips on my forehead. "Take care, Cherry G." He laughed, the sound brittle. "I miss you already."

He began to move past me, and I grabbed his arm. He stopped, looking down. "What?"

I gave in to everything I was feeling. Wanting.

Him.

I flung my arms around his neck, and I kissed him.

## DOM

Jesus, her mouth. I knew it would be addictive. Despite the snappy words, the constant denials, and her bitter tone at times, I knew she'd be sweet. The perfect aphrodisiac.

She whimpered as I slid my tongue along hers. Clutched at my neck as the kiss deepened, our tongues exploring, lips devouring, and taste buds on overdrive.

I groaned as she tugged on my hair. Bent and lifted her into my arms, backing her into the wall. She wrapped her legs around me, biting at my lips. Begged me silently for more.

Which I was happy to give her.

It didn't matter we were in a bar. In a hallway. That her daughter and my coworker were around. All that mattered was she'd finally given in. Finally let me touch her. Kiss her.

And now, I wanted more.

I pulled back, meeting her dazed eyes. "I'm taking you home, Cherry G."

She pulled my face back to hers. "Tell me what you're going to do to me," she begged in a quiet whisper.

"I'm going to fuck you. Claim you. Make love to you. I'm going to take you hard. Then slow. Then both. I'm going to ruin you for anyone else." I pressed my forehead to hers. "Tell me that I can."

"Yes. *Oh God, yes.*"

"And it's not only going to be tonight," I promised. "Once we do this, you're mine. You understand me? I don't share. Ever. And especially you."

She rolled her hips into me, and I fisted her hair, kissing her again. "Patience, pretty lady. You do that again, and all bets are off. We need to get somewhere private. I want to take my time with you."

"Take me home, Dom. Please."

A slow grin pulled at my lips. "You said Dom." I kissed her hard. "You'll be screaming it soon."

I lowered her feet to the floor, holding her until she was steady. I smoothed her hair back, smiling down at her. "You're a mess."

"So are you."

"Do you care?"

"No."

I took her lips again. "We're heading right out. Okay?"

"Yes." She cleared her throat. "We have to try to act natural around Hannah. I don't want her to think—"

I covered her mouth with mine again. "Too late, lady. She's gonna know."

Then I tugged her behind me, heading to the table. Chase and Hannah were staring at us, Hannah's eyes wide with shock as she took in her mother's disheveled appearance. I wasn't trying to hide my erection either. I couldn't.

I stopped at the table, grabbing Cherry's purse and my jacket. "We're going for coffee," I said, my voice deep and rough. I looked at Hannah. "Don't wait up."

Cherry looked at her daughter, wide-eyed and blushing. "Just coffee," she called over her shoulder. "I'll be home soon."

I laughed loudly. "Don't count on it!" I yelled back.

She'd be lucky if I let her go at all.

# CHAPTER FIVE

## Dom

I n the car, I held her hand, and she gripped mine back. I had to maintain some sort of physical contact with her. Every time I glanced over, she was watching me, her eyes wide. Then she started talking. Nonstop. She commented on how long it took to get out of the parking lot. The number of people around. The interior of my car. How nice my leather jacket was. How she'd always wanted one but thought she was too old.

It took me a few moments to realize her nattering was her way of handling her nerves. It was rather endearing.

I pulled into the driveway of the place I was renting, grateful it was a short trip from the bar. I went to her side, tugging her from the vehicle and, before she could say anything else, swooping her into my arms. She grasped at my shoulders with a shocked gasp.

"I can walk."

"Not fast enough."

At the door, I paused. "It's 4-3-0-0. Type it in."

She did as I instructed, and the door unlocked with a

snap. I took her inside, heading straight to my bedroom. The door clicked shut behind me, the lock reengaging.

In my room, I set her on her feet and stared down at her. Nerves had replaced that look of desire from earlier. The want was gone, and worry took its place. She looked around. "This is nice. The rooms are a good size—"

I cupped her face between my hands and bent, kissing her, silencing her. Endearing as it was, I didn't need a running commentary of my rental. I needed her mouth. Her desire.

I let her set the pace, slowly deepening the kiss as her passion blossomed. I wanted her with me. In the moment. Lost to everything but me. Us.

She was tense at first, then her shoulders slackened. Her body softened, pressing into me. She wrapped her arms around my neck, sliding her tongue along mine in sensuous passes. Low whimpers escaped her lips, her breathy sighs warming my skin.

I held her close, further deepening the kiss, claiming her mouth. She shivered in my arms as I pulled on her pretty blouse, tugging it over her head, breaking away from her mouth long enough to get it off her. It caught and I heard a seam tear, but neither of us stopped. She pulled at my T-shirt, frowning as if it offended her by being on me, and I helped her rid me of it. I took her mouth again, sliding my hands up to cup her full breasts, stroking the hard nipples through the lace under my fingers. Seconds later, the lace was gone, her bare skin filling my hands. The weight of her warm breasts was perfection. Piece by piece, our clothing was discarded, our bodies close together as we kissed and touched. I bent, lifting her again, and she wrapped her legs around me. I groaned at the feel of her, hot and slick against my cock, and I ground against her, wanting her to feel my desire.

"I'm not on birth control," she murmured. "I went through early menopause."

"I'm safe, but I have condoms."

She hesitated.

"I'm not a player, Cherry. It's been over a year."

"I can't remember how long it's been for me," she whispered.

"We'll use them."

She shook her head, taking a deep breath. "I-I trust you."

I cupped her face. "That means so much to me. Thank you."

I walked to the bed, laying her on her back and stepping away, admiring the view. Her beautiful hair spread out on my plain comforter. Her full breasts moved rapidly as she struggled to keep her breathing regular. Her nipples were stiff, and I wanted to taste them. Her hips were rounded, and she kept her legs together modestly, that blush I liked spreading across her skin. Her chest, even her stomach, was flushed.

I shook my head in wonder. "Look at you."

"I'm not young and pretty," she whispered.

"Young, no. Pretty isn't the right word either," I agreed. "Beautiful. Sexy. Perfect for me. God, I want to feast on you."

She blinked, then sat up, taking my cock in her hand. I groaned as she stroked me, meeting my eyes, defiant and confident. "I want to taste you too."

I barely held in my groan. "Ladies first."

She wrapped her lips around me. It was all I could do not to fist her hair and fuck her mouth. I was fascinated as I watched my cock slide between her full lips. Felt her tongue wrap around me. She watched me watching her, and, unable to stop myself, I wound a handful of hair around my fist, pumping into her mouth. "Such a good girl," I purred. "Look at you sucking my cock. You like that, Cherry? If I touched you right now, I bet you'd be wet, wouldn't you?" I growled at her. She nodded, humming, setting off another wave of pleasure through my body.

"Show me," I demanded.

She slipped a hand between her legs, holding up her fingers. They glistened in the low light coming from the hall. I grabbed her hand, sucking, as she whimpered low in her throat.

"You taste delicious, and I can't wait anymore," I hissed, tugging on her hair. "My turn."

She swirled her tongue, sucking one last time, then moved her head back, my cock resting on her bottom lip. She kissed the tip, tonguing the slit, and I groaned.

"You are trouble, Cherry G."

I lifted her under her arms and tossed her farther back on the bed. I gripped her knees, opening her to me. She looked uncertain, and I shook my head. "You are beautiful. Lying there, wet and ready for me. I could slide in and fuck you as hard as I wanted right now, couldn't I?" I demanded. "You're soaked." I ran a finger along her, teasing and light. "But I want to taste you first. Make you come with my mouth. Then my fingers. Then you get my cock."

She whimpered, her legs falling open wider. Her nipples begged for my mouth, and I tongued them, biting and sucking until they were stiff points and wet from my teasing. Then I moved down her body, kissing and licking. I picked up her foot, kissing the arch, up to her knee, then did the same with the other. She was almost panting by the time I buried my face into her center and licked. She bowed her back off her bed with a low cry as I circled her clit with slow passes of my tongue. She curled her hands into fists on the bedding, twisting the material as I stroked, licked, sucked, and nibbled. Slid in one finger, then added another, pumping fast as she began to stiffen.

"Come for me, Cherry. Come all over my hand," I praised her. "So fucking beautiful. Look at you."

She cried out, her eyes going wide, her muscles tightening.

I hovered over her, settling between her thighs and slamming into her. That set off another orgasm, this time my name flying from her lips as she choked my cock, the sensation incredible. I slid my arms around her, lifting her to my chest and covering her mouth with mine, kissing her hard. She gripped my shoulders, grasped at my biceps, and dug her nails into my back. Our mouths were fused together, our breaths mingling. I grabbed her perfect ass, moving her with me. The bed shifted with the force of our coupling. Sweat rolled down our torsos, our skin gliding together. I gripped her hip with one hand, the other wrapped around her hair and pressing into her back. I had never experienced such intense sensations with anyone before. Never felt the need to be as close to someone. To feel them molded around me. Everything with Cherry was magnified.

Including the strength of the orgasm I felt beginning to take over. Fire spread through me, hot and bright. My cock swelled, and I thrust into the heat and wet of her, needing to be as deeply embedded as I could be.

"Dom!" she gasped, tearing her mouth from mine. "Oh my God, again. More!"

I exploded, pleasure overtaking my body. I held her tight to my chest, letting the sensations flood me. She whimpered my name over and over, her lips by my ear, her breath hot on my skin. I moved until I was sated. Exhausted.

Wondering what the hell had just happened.

We stilled, our skin cooling, our breathing returning to normal. I slid a finger under her chin, lifting her face. I pressed a kiss to her full lips. "Wow."

She looked up, her gaze soft, warm, and emotional. "Wow is right."

"You okay, pretty lady?"

"I'm good."

I eased her back to the mattress and slid out of her, grimacing as I rested beside her. She shifted, placing her head on my chest, draping her arm across my stomach.

"I should go?" she said in the form of a question.

"Nope. You're staying right here. I'm not done with you yet."

"Oh."

I kissed her forehead. "Sleep a bit. I'm not going anywhere." I held her tighter. "Neither are you."

"Hannah—"

"Knows where you are. That you're safe. She's also fully aware you're a grown woman. I highly doubt she's shocked. Besides, the way she and Chase were eyeing each other up, I doubt she's even thinking of you right now. Pretty sure the headboard is slamming into the wall loudly."

She slapped my chest, even as she laughed. "Stop. That is my daughter."

"Another grown woman. Both of you satisfied."

She lifted her head, a smile on her lips. "Did I say I was satisfied yet, Dom?"

I wasn't sure what shocked me more. Her teasing, or the way my cock got on board so quickly.

Cherry was obviously my own personal Viagra.

I could live with that.

The room was quiet as we recovered from round two. Cherry was draped over my chest, her fingers tracing lazy patterns on my skin.

"Who hurt you, Cherry?" I asked quietly.

She stiffened, then sighed.

"About two years after Mike died, I was lonely. Sad. Weary. So tired of working and being the only one, trying to raise Hannah, go to work, handle the bills. Everything."

"I imagine it was hard."

"It was. I met a man. He was a salesman for a big roofing distributor in the region. He seemed great. Said all the right things. Did all the right things. Asked about my daughter. Showed an interest in her and me. Suddenly, I wasn't so lonely."

"What happened?"

"He was on the road a lot, but he kept in touch. Brought us gifts. I started relying on him. Trusting him. Falling for him." She huffed out a long breath. "Until his wife showed up at my door. Told me the truth. He had me and another woman on the side."

"Wow. Busy man."

"The worst part was that Hannah was involved. It was hard enough to deal with knowing he'd lied to me, but involving my child was inexcusable. Knowing I had slept with a married man horrified me."

"You didn't know."

"I should have."

I tightened my hold on her. "Stop blaming yourself for his actions. You didn't know."

"She lived in Niagara Falls. I lived in Toronto. The

other girlfriend was in Belleville. He had a large territory that he routinely traveled. He made sure to have company everywhere. His schedule was pretty set, so no one questioned his absences. He played it and us very well."

"And after that?"

"It took me a long time to trust again. The next guy was an absolute player. Charming. Handsome. And a lying sack of shit. After that, I gave up and concentrated on Hannah."

I chuckled. "Well, I am neither married nor a liar." I pressed a kiss to her head. "Nor a player."

"I know," she admitted. "It was my own insecurities. It seemed every guy I dated or was introduced to had an agenda."

"Oh, I have one, Cherry G. I want you. I want you in my life. I want to be part of yours. That is my whole agenda, and I am happy for you to know it."

She snuggled closer. "I kinda like that."

"Good." I lifted her chin and captured her mouth. "Because I'm not going anywhere."

I woke up in the early morning light, Cherry asleep beside me, her hand on my chest. All night, we stayed in physical contact. Snuggled close under the blankets. At times, she was draped over me. Others, I spooned her. But even if we rolled apart, somehow we touched, our hands clasping or resting against the other person. I shifted, studying her in the low light. Asleep, she looked sweet—soft and vulnerable. All traits I knew she carried in her but would never allow the world to see. She was proud, independent, and strong. I liked all those things about her. The hidden parts and the ones she let the world view. She was complex.

Alluring. Like a puzzle I needed to solve. I planned on doing so and enjoying every moment of it.

I was sorry for the bad times she'd been through. The assholes who'd hurt her. I was determined to show her I was in this for the long haul. From the moment I met her, I was captivated. And that intensity hadn't worn off now that we had slept together. It had, in fact, grown stronger. I wanted to be that man for her. The one she could trust and rely on.

I pushed a stray curl behind her ear, grinning as another fell and took its place on her cheek. Her curls were as soft as I'd thought they would be. I loved how they felt fisted in my hand, tickling my thighs as she rode me, her head bent back as she cried out in desire.

I had never experienced such passion with a woman until last night—the kind that drove all rational thought from your mind and focused your attention on a single image. The person in front of you. Everything in me had wanted her pleasure. Her cries. Her mouth and body. Her whispered pleas and whimpers of desire. Nothing but complete bliss and being inside her could cool my ardor.

Even that hadn't been enough. Once I'd had her, I wanted her again. I woke her three times in the night to sate my desire.

And still, it raged.

I lifted up on my elbow, watching her. I traced a finger down her creamy skin, tugging at the blanket covering her. I tried not to grin at the marks on her neck, the traces of love bites that lingered there and on her breasts. The swollen pink of her mouth from mine. I felt the slight sting from her fingernails embedded in my skin at the height of our passion. The ache growing in my cock at the sight of her resting beside me, unknowingly waking the animal in me simply by being there, close, sweet, and inviting.

I lowered my head, sucking a nipple into my mouth. It grew taut and wet under my tongue, and a breathy sigh escaped Cherry's mouth, the air moving my hair. She murmured my name, curling her hand into my hair as I turned my attention to her other breast, giving it the same treatment as I rolled her wet nipple between my fingers. I rose over her, settling between her legs.

Her eyes were still closed, but her body responded, opening to me like a flower. Her heat surrounded me as I slid my cock along her wet pussy, watching her the whole time. Her eyes blinked open, widening when she saw me, but she wrapped her legs around my hips, drawing me in. I slid inside her, groaning at how right it felt. How right we felt.

Without a word, I kissed her, moving in long, slow passes. She made a strangled noise in her throat, her arms holding me tight. I opened my eyes, meeting her wide gaze. I kept moving, our gazes never faltering, our mouths staying together. I slid my hands along her arms, lifting them over her head, holding them with one hand as I gripped her ass with the other, moving faster, my need for her becoming intense. She gasped as I changed the angle, and she began to breathe faster.

Everything narrowed down to the feel of where we were joined. The connection between us. The spiral of ecstasy and the heat of our bodies as we moved together. She stiffened, her fingers crushing mine as she orgasmed, the clutch of her sending me over the edge. I was free-falling, not caring if I hit the ground. Pure, unadulterated elation flowed through me. It wound around us, a fire that could not be stopped.

Until we were nothing but ashes.

And I was okay with that.

We dozed, woke again, showering away the desire of the night from our bodies but not our minds. Cherry was oddly shy again, which made me smile. The running commentary began as I made coffee as she perched on one of the high stools by the counter that separated the kitchen from the living room. My cupboards were pretty, the layout nice. She loved the wooden floors and the old crown molding.

"So charming," she stated, taking a sip of her coffee, allowing me the chance to speak.

"Charming is one word," I snorted. "Add in the leaking pipes, drafty windows, and squeaking floors, and I can think of another one."

"But that lovely tub."

I met her gaze. "Really, Cherry G, do I look like a tub guy?"

"I suppose not. But one never knows."

"I think after last night—and this morning—you know me pretty well. At least in one sense." I winked at her.

She tossed her hair, making me smile. "For all I know, you could enjoy a good soak."

I took a long drink of my coffee, eyeing her. She wore my shirt, the long sleeves rolled up, the bottom coming halfway down her thighs. Her hair was damp, curling softly around her face in long waves. In the morning light, free of makeup or proper clothes, she was effortlessly sexy. Pretty. I liked her. A lot.

"I do like a good soak," I drawled. "Namely, my cock bathed in your hot pussy. But other than that, I'm a shower guy."

Her cheeks flamed, and I had to chuckle. She tried to

divert the conversation, pointing out the pluses of my gas stove.

I poured another coffee and let her ramble.

Used to the silence of my own company, I found myself enjoying it.

"You ripped my blouse," Cherry said, her voice prim.

"Wear the shirt you have on now," I replied, not at all put out. "I like how it looks on you."

"I liked that blouse."

"I'll buy you another one. It was in the way of your skin."

She made an exasperated sound. "Hannah will notice."

I had to laugh. "Hannah has already figured it out, Cherry G. She knows her momma was up to no good all night. The two of you can probably share notes."

Her indignant sigh said it all.

"Chase invited us to join them. You want to do that or head back to bed?" I appraised her in a long, slow glance. "I know what I'd prefer."

She slid off the stool, crossing her arms. "I want to see my daughter, then I'm heading back to Toronto."

I sidled over, standing in front of her. "You want me to follow, baby?"

"Follow?"

"I can come back with you. Spend the evening. The night. You can show me all the great things about your place."

She blinked. "You-you want to come with me? You're not tired of me?"

I shook my head, looping my arms around her waist. "I

doubt that is ever gonna happen. Certainly not now. Not today. I can't get enough of you."

All her tension melted, her body conforming itself to mine. Her eyes grew softer, filling with an emotion I couldn't identify, but I liked. She wrapped her arms around my neck. "Really?"

I lowered my head, my lips ghosting over hers. "Really."

She yanked me close, licking at my mouth. "Then, yes."

# CHAPTER SIX

## Dom

W e pulled up outside Chase's, heading to the front door. Cherry looked nervous again, worrying the inside of her cheek and pausing on the step. "Maybe I should just call you later," she offered. "I'm going to get my things and head home."

I shook my head, amused. "No way, pretty lady. I'm coming in with you."

She narrowed her eyes. "That is my daughter in there."

I nodded. "A grown woman. Yes."

Cherry spun on her heel and walked in, pushing the door partially closed behind her. I laughed low in my chest, her movements amusing rather than insulting. She was acting like a teenager sneaking home from a date and hoping not to be caught. I knew it was way too late for that.

"Morning, kids!" Chase sang out, appearing in the hall. "We got breakfast on the table. Come on in, Dom. No need to stand outside like a degenerate or something."

"Dom was just leaving," Cherry protested, the color on her cheeks high.

"Breakfast?" I said at the same time.

"Fresh cinnamon rolls from Lulu's."

"He'll take one to go," Cherry babbled.

I shook my head with a wide grin. "I'll eat in." I enjoyed seeing her distracted and trying to get rid of me.

Cherry huffed an impatient sound and brushed past Chase, hurrying into the kitchen. Chase met my grin with one of his own. "Good night?"

I shut the door behind me. "It was incredible, but keep that between us." I met his eyes. "Be respectful. I'm trying to win her over."

"Scout's honor."

I hung my head. "Well, I'm fucked."

Laughing, he clapped me on the shoulder. "It's all good."

In the kitchen, Chase offered me a cup of coffee. I took it from him, looking toward the Gallagher women. Cherry and Hannah were talking, quietly and fast, their heads bent together. They were both gesturing, their hands flying around as they spoke, the motions similar. Cherry looked flushed and nervous. Hannah looked slightly horrified.

"You're looking at your future," I muttered to Chase. "Good Lord, that woman can talk. I had to get inventive in order to keep her quiet."

Chase sputtered into his cup, side-eyeing me. I winked, not at all embarrassed.

"Shut up, yourself," he muttered, pushing the buns my way. "Fill your mouth with one of those instead."

I grinned, taking a bite. "Not as sweet as what I filled it with earlier."

Cherry heard me, her head snapping in my direction. I winked at her. "Yes, Cherry G. I'm talking about you."

"Well, stop it," she and Hannah said at the same time.

Chase laughed, and I joined in. They looked so alike, acted the same.

"Sweet buns?" he asked Cherry, lifting the plate. "Or did you get enough of Dom's?"

Cherry's eyes widened. I chuckled, and Hannah glared at Chase. Cherry took one, primly thanking him. Then she and Hannah began talking again, ignoring our presence. We sipped and chewed in silence for a moment, then talked about a few things on his mind.

Cherry tossed her hair at something Hannah said, and Chase chuckled. Cherry had a bite mark at the base of her neck, and Hannah's eyes focused on the mark before she met Chase's gaze with a WTF look. Chase winked at her, and she bit her lip, holding in her laughter. I was barely able to contain mine.

"What?" Cherry asked.

"Ah, you have a little, um, mark," Chase said. "On your neck."

She brushed at her skin. "Where?"

"The spot I sank my teeth into," I said calmly. "It'll fade. Until next time."

Cherry's eyes widened, and she looked at Hannah.

"Mom…" Hannah choked out.

Cherry stood. "I'm going to get ready to head home. I have a million things to do." She practically ran from the kitchen. Hannah began to stand, but I waved her off.

"I'll go talk to her." I paused at the door, turning to speak. "I like your mother, Hannah. She's incredible. You should come have lunch with me. Get to know me better. I plan on being around a lot." I glanced down the hall. "If that stubborn woman will let me," I added, flexing my shoulders. "I'm going in." I flashed a smile. "If you hear screaming, no one is being hurt. Trust me. Don't come in."

Then I followed Cherry. I had a feeling that was going to happen a lot in our relationship.

Might as well get used to it now.

## CHERRY

Late Wednesday afternoon, I sipped a cup of tea, resting my head in one hand as I relaxed back into the chair. I had cleaned my little apartment, done my errands and laundry. I was ready for the week ahead. Since I was working on Saturday, I had today off. I always liked doing my errands on the weekdays since the stores weren't as busy as the weekend. My phone buzzed, and I looked at the text from Hannah asking if I wanted to come out on the weekend after work and help her with her garden. She was so excited in her new home. With Chase. It was obvious to me my daughter had fallen hard and fast for the young man. I had to admit, I liked him a lot. He was caring, hardworking, and as serious about her as she was about him. I could see the way he watched her. It reminded me of the way my husband used to watch me. There was an underlying intensity to the glances. A way of making sure I was okay if I wasn't beside him. A longing to have me back and close.

The same way Dom looked at me now.

Dominic Salvatore.

I couldn't get the man off my mind. No matter how hard I tried. After my husband died, I never thought I would feel such an intense attraction for another man. After the one huge mistake, years had passed, some casual dates occurred, attempted relationships—nothing. But with

Dom, it was powerful. Hot. Yearning. I scoffed out loud as I realized I was missing him even now.

Our night together had been passionate. Incredible. He awoke the woman in me, bringing back the lust and desire I had thought were gone for good. Simply seeing him in the bar had caused a reaction I didn't expect. Longing. Heat. Even jealousy at the looks other women were bestowing on him. And as hard as I tried to fight it, I wanted him. He seemed to enjoy our sparring, egging me on until I broke, kissing him with a fiery passion I didn't know I possessed.

I passed a hand over my head. I was still torn. Unsure. I wasn't interested in booty calls and the occasional weekend fling. He insisted that wasn't what he wanted either, but how would a long-distance relationship work?

He had walked into the guest room on Sunday, pulling me into his arms and kissing me until I was a shaking mess. He cupped my face, staring down at me with those incredible eyes.

*"You obviously need some space, so I won't follow you home. But I'll see you this week, Cherry G. And the one after. I'm not going anywhere, so get used to it."*

*"Do I have a choice in this?"* I asked.

*He smiled. "Tell me to leave, and I'll go. But mean it."*

The thought of not seeing him again kept me quiet. He laughed low in his chest, the sound pleased. *"I know you didn't expect me,"* he said, suddenly serious. *"I didn't expect you either, but I'm damn glad it happened. We'll figure it all out. Stop overthinking, worrying, and reacting to every other negative thought in your head. Stay in the moment with me."*

Then he kissed me again and left.

Hannah came in to see me as I zipped up my little overnight bag.

*"You okay, Mom?"*

"I'm fine."

She sat on the bed. "You're attracted to him, aren't you?"

I sighed and nodded. "I shouldn't be."

"Why?" she asked. "Because of Dad?"

"No," I replied, sitting beside her. "Your father would have wanted me to move on, and it has been years. But Dom isn't the sort of person I would have expected to have a relationship with."

"You mean because he is sort of a bad boy?" Hannah teased. "You think an accountant would be a better fit?"

I laughed. "He is so incredibly hot," I admitted. "Not what I expected."

"Did you sleep with him?" she asked.

I looked her straight in the eye. "Not a lot of sleep happened, Hannah."

She laughed. "You like him."

"He's not my type," I insisted. "He's a reformed bad boy who hasn't completely given up that edge," I mused. "He's bossy and determined. Dom is the right name for him. He gets what he wants." I paused. "Everywhere."

"I see," she murmured.

"But he is so sweet," I mused. "Thoughtful. Giving. I haven't felt like a sexy woman in years. Since your dad. Last night, I was reminded of the fact that I was." I swallowed. "Several times."

"Um…"

I kept talking. "And he came in here and reminded me again."

Hannah's eyes widened in horror, and I waved my hand. "We didn't. But the man can kiss. And what a dirty talker." I fanned myself. "My, my, my."

She laughed again, and I had to grin. It felt as if our roles were reversed. I was the lovestruck teenager, and she was the one giving me advice. "If you like him and he likes you, why are you fighting it?"

"He lives here. I live in Toronto. I am too old to be a casual hookup, whenever-you're-in-town woman. I don't want that."

"Is that what Dom wants? He seems pretty steady."

*"Long-distance relationships are too hard, jellybean."*

*"Not if you really want them."*

*I shrugged. "I'm not sure I do."*

*Hannah stood. "Be honest with yourself, Mom. And allow yourself the chance to be happy. Be it for now or longer. I like Dom. Chase does too. Maybe you need to give him a chance. Give yourself a chance."*

Her words were on a constant loop in my head. When she was little, I had to put myself and my wants and needs on a back burner. Working, making sure she was healthy, warm, and cared for were my number one priorities. I had forgotten what it was like to give in to what I wanted. My entire world had revolved around Hannah and her needs.

Dom's observations flitted through my head. *"She's a grown woman,"* he had pointed out on more than one occasion.

He was right. I knew that. My head knew that, but at times, my heart still thought of her as my little girl. Maybe I needed to listen to Hannah, to Dom—and put myself and my wants first for a change. I stood, wandering to the kitchen and checking out the contents of the refrigerator for dinner. I hated cooking for myself. Eating alone constantly. I missed Hannah and her company. I missed having someone around.

Dom's image ran through my head. He wanted to be around. The truth was, I enjoyed his company. I wouldn't mind spending more time with him.

Was I ready to do that?

I wasn't used to putting myself first. What I needed, what I wanted, always came second. To Hannah. To my business. To what the world demanded of me.

Perhaps it was time for a change. He certainly seemed to want that.

Every day, I got a text from him—often more than one.

He dropped little tidbits of himself into them, often referred to our night together, but, more importantly, checked in on me.

DOM

> Hope your day was good. I was thinking of you, so mine was.

> It feels like years since I kissed you. How has it only been 2 days? I need to rectify that. I miss you, Cherry G.

Or last night's…

DOM

> My sheets still smell like you. Us. I like falling asleep to your scent. But I prefer falling asleep with you beside me. Let's make that happen.

Sometimes, I responded. Other times, his words left me so overwhelmed, I couldn't find a way to reply. Sometimes, I was so breathless, nothing formed but a sense of desire and longing so intense, I wasn't sure how to handle it.

My buzzer rang out, startling me. I shut the fridge door and crossed over to the front door. I wasn't expecting anyone or a delivery, and I was too short for the peephole to do me much good.

"Hello?" I asked.

"Cherry G, it's me. Open up."

"Dom?" I said, surprised and frankly delighted.

"You have other men calling you Cherry G?" He paused, his voice becoming gravelly. "You have other men visiting you?"

I tried to tamp down the thrill that shot through me at his words. His possessive tone. Not even my husband had been possessive. He had been too laid-back and friendly to

74

act that way. Dom was the exact opposite of Mike. In every single way.

"You gonna let me in, woman?" he growled.

Laughing, I flipped the lock and opened the door, stepping back and bracing myself. Still, the sight of him made me inhale quickly.

He wore his usual jeans and leather jacket. A blue T-shirt stretched across his chest. He carried a bag and a bouquet of flowers. His Doc Martens were dusty, his jeans tight, and his expression intense. Yet his eyes were soft as they met mine. His gaze was focused on me and me alone. He stopped in front of me, swooping down without a word and capturing my mouth. His kiss was powerful. Drugging. I whimpered into his mouth as he wrapped his arm around my waist, pulling me close. I felt the scrape of his scruff along my jaw. The fullness of his lips on mine. His minty fresh taste. His manly scent that wrapped around me as tight as his embrace. His long exhale of air, as if he'd been waiting to breathe until he kissed me. As if he couldn't live without doing so.

He pulled back, cupping my face. "Hello, Cherry G."

"Hi," I replied, breathless. "I-I wasn't expecting you."

"I told you I'd see you this week. Chase mentioned Hannah said you had today off. I thought I'd give you a break and come make you dinner." He winked as he strode past me. "And these flowers are for you." He deposited the large bouquet in my arms.

"You cook?" I asked, dumbfounded.

"Of course I do. I'm a single guy. I can't survive on takeout."

He took off his jacket, the muscles in his arms rippling, making his tattoos stand out. "I hope you like steak, Cherry G, because that's what's on the menu."

"I do."

"Great. Now, shut the door and come sit down. Tell me about your day."

I watched Dom move around with the confidence of a man used to being in the kitchen. He located the wineglasses and corkscrew and poured us each a glass of wine, then got busy, rubbing spices into two thick steaks, prepping potatoes, and, with another wink, pouring a salad into a bowl. "I cook," he said with a grin. "But it's simple. I use a lot of shortcuts."

"Still beats takeout every day."

He nodded. "It gets tiresome after a while. I enjoy a meal out, the occasional pizza or Chinese in, but I like good, homemade food. I taught myself the basics."

I set the table, easing around him as he moved. He was in control and smooth as he worked. He turned as I sidled past, pulling me close and kissing my neck. "You smell so good," he murmured. "Right here, especially," he added, nosing my collar out of the way.

I shivered. "You're supposed to be cooking."

"Oh, baby, believe me, I am." He bit down playfully. "I'm boiling up for you."

I laughed at his cheesy remark, but for some reason, I wound my arms around his waist and held him tight. He tossed the utensil in his hand to the counter and spun me in his arms, humming in my ear. We danced around my small kitchen, holding each other, him humming, me smiling. It was ridiculous—and fun.

Then he twirled me away and shook his head, muttering about distractions. Without thinking, I reached out and cupped his cheek, stroking the skin. "I like being your distraction," I whispered. "I'm glad you're here."

His eyes crinkled in delight, and he turned his head, kissing my palm. "Me too, baby. Me too."

Not long after, we sat down to eat. I had added a candle, and he lit it, turning the kitchen lights down low. He had music playing on his phone, and we talked as we ate, me complimenting him on his dinner. The steak was tender and delicious, the baked potatoes fluffy and overflowing with butter and sour cream. Even the salad was tasty.

"I don't remember the last time someone cooked for me, aside from Hannah," I murmured, looking at my plate. "And usually, those meals are a joint collaboration."

He sliced off a piece of steak, holding his fork to my mouth. "Open, Cherry G. Let me feed you."

My lips parted, and he slipped the steak in, cutting himself a larger piece and chewing. I closed my eyes as the flavors of the meat, the butter, garlic, and rosemary he'd basted the steak with, burst on my taste buds.

"Oh God. So good."

He grinned. "I guess you'll keep me around then, huh?"

I tried to hide my returning smile as I cut into my own steak. Teasingly, I held out my fork. "Do I get to feed you, Dom?"

With a low growl, he leaned in, gripping the back of my neck and pulling my face close. He kissed me hard. Deep. Then he pulled back, his chest working hard.

"You already do, Cherry G. You already do."

I had no words to respond to him. With a wink, he gripped my wrist then closed his lips around my fork, taking the piece of steak I offered. His voice was rough and low when he spoke.

"Almost as good as you."

I reached for my wine. I had a feeling I was going to

need it.

# CHAPTER SEVEN

## Cherry

Neither of us spoke much during dinner. The odd comment, lots of looks passing between us. He was different tonight. Always intense, he had an underlying sense of unease or sadness about him. It was reflected in his eyes at times. I longed to ask him, but I had a feeling he wasn't ready to talk. But I also sensed what was bothering him might have led to this impromptu visit. I knew I had to be patient. When he was ready to talk, he would. Hannah was much the same way, and I had learned when to push and when not to.

We finished dinner and sat back, sipping the last of the wine.

"I didn't bring dessert," he mused. "I didn't think."

"I can handle that," I said with a grin. "It's covered." I stood, taking our plates. "I'll tidy up and make coffee. You sit and tell me about your day this time."

He stopped me with a hand on my waist. He gazed up at me, and once again, I saw the sadness lurking in his eyes. But he smiled and tugged me down, kissing me gently. "This dinner has been the best part of it," he murmured.

I kissed him back, unable to hug him since my hands were full. "Mine too," I admitted.

"Getting used to me?" he teased.

I shrugged. "A little."

He grinned and pushed me away. "Get to work."

I put on the coffee to brew and tidied up. There wasn't much since Dom cleaned as he cooked. I put the dishes in the small portable dishwasher in the corner, rinsed out the pan he'd used for the steaks, and wiped down the counter as he talked. He told me a funny story about a customer in the garage that made me laugh.

"She insisted she wanted the 'good air' for her tires. She told us the garage she'd used in Toronto kept it special for her. She even showed us the bill."

"I assume she knows nothing about cars."

He shook his head. "Maxx explained it to her and the fact that she'd been ripped off for a couple of years. When she found out there shouldn't be a charge for filling her tires, she was upset. Maxx went through all her bills. They'd charged her for all sorts of things. Extra thick oil, extended warranty spark plugs—the list went on. Charly was so incensed that she called the garage while the customer was there and tore them a new asshole. They agreed to refund some of her money, but not enough. She advised the customer to go to the Better Business Bureau with a complaint."

"How did she find you?"

"She was driving by, and her tire pressure light came on. Maxx thinks they were underfilling her tires purposely so she would go and they would 'top them up.' She was paying a monthly maintenance fee for it since they told her that was the cheapest route. Maxx—all of us—hates to see people, especially women, get ripped off. He convinced her to come to the classes we hold so she could understand her car better. She's young and pretty and, frankly, clueless—an easy target."

I carried the coffee to the table and set it down with a couple of plates. I bent and kissed him. "She's lucky she found you guys."

His eyes crinkled in pleasure at my statement.

"Now, don't laugh when you see dessert."

"Okay."

I opened the refrigerator, taking out a small box. I slid the contents onto a plate and set it on the table. Dom stared at the small birthday cake in silence. "What is that?" he asked, his voice sounding strangled.

I sat down, meeting his gaze. It was pain-filled and shocked. I was confused.

"My local bakery makes cakes. If one isn't bought, she reduces them. I can never resist a white bakery cake. It cuts into two easily, so I treat myself on occasion." I paused, noticing the fact that his hands had begun to shake. "Dom, what is it?"

"I can't…" he choked.

I took the cake and put it back in the fridge. He stood and crossed to the living room, pulling his hands through his hair. I walked up behind him, sliding my arms around him, puzzled as to why the sight of a small birthday cake would cause him such sadness. "I'm sorry."

He turned and wrapped me in his arms. "It's not your fault. I didn't expect that. I was trying to forget, to let it be another day, but then the cake—" He stopped, his embrace tightening. I rested my head on his chest, listening to his heartbeat gallop.

"What about the cake?" I asked.

"Today is my son's birthday," he replied quietly after a moment. "Another one of his birthdays I'm not part of."

"Oh, Dom," I whispered, shocked at his words. "I'm so sorry."

I looked up, meeting his troubled gaze. "Do you want to tell me?"

His eyes met mine, the pain in his gaze now obvious to see. Heartbreak was written all over his features.

"I'll listen if you want. If not, I understand."

He let out a long exhale of air. "I want to tell you. I never talk about it. But with you, Cherry, I want that."

I stepped back, taking his hand and leading him to the sofa. "Then tell me."

The room was quiet for a few moments as Dom gathered his thoughts. He looked as if he was going to talk a couple of times, then stopped. I wondered if he was unsure how to start, so I decided to ask him a few questions.

"I didn't know you had a son."

"I don't talk about him."

"Is he about Hannah's age?"

"No. He's much younger. He—Josh—is thirteen today."

"Oh," I said. "Much younger."

"I met his mother when I was thirty-four. She got pregnant and had Josh when I was thirty-five." He rubbed a hand over his scruff. "Our relationship wasn't a good one. She was incredibly demanding and self-centered. Manipulative. Nasty when cornered. I broke it off after a particularly bad fight. She found out she was pregnant and told me. I wanted to be part of my kid's life, so we got back together. Her pregnancy somehow made her softer, and we got along better. I thought things would be okay."

"But they weren't."

He shook his head. "I loved being a dad. Everything about it—even the diapers. Roxanne was a good mom, and things were all right for a while. Then slowly, she began the mind games again. The demands. The constant emotional upheaval. I was to blame for everything in her life she hated."

"How awful to live like that."

He shut his eyes, his hands curling into fists on his thighs. I reached over and laid my hand on his, and he stared down, opening his fingers and flipping his palm over so I could grip his hand. I stroked the skin as he began to talk again.

"I stayed for Josh. I loved him, and I couldn't bear to think of my life without him. But she was done with me and made my life miserable. She told me she wanted me gone, and I said I'd take Josh with me." He stopped for a moment. "She was awful to me, but she was a loving mom to him. I couldn't fault her that. But I hated the thought of my son growing up in such a toxic environment. She refused to let me take him. We argued and fought. She berated me constantly. Made me doubt every decision. The only peace I had was rocking him to sleep or sleeping on the floor by his crib. I left to stop the horrendous atmosphere. She got a slimy lawyer and a bunch of friends who swore that I was a deadbeat dad and did nothing. That I refused to marry her and settle down. I got a lawyer and had a few people to vouch for me too, but hers played dirty. I lost and got limited visitation, while she had full custody. I paid my child support monthly and saw Josh as much as I was allowed. Then one day, she got married. Informed me they were moving. Again, I fought and lost. Josh was three at the time. They moved to Simcoe, making it harder for me to see Josh. We fought all the time over visitation. When I would get him, he was difficult and cried to go home. The visits were awful. I think she filled his head with stories about me. Bad ones. At times, I thought he was afraid of me. Then I was informed they were moving out of province. I tried to fight it and lost. She used all the missed visitations against me, and I lost Josh." He paused. "She even went so far as to say I might not be his father."

"What?"

"She said she had an affair and that Josh might not be mine. I refused to believe that. He looked like me—he had my eyes. I demanded a paternity test, and she backed off. But it shook me. I doubted the truth for a while, even while I knew in my heart he was mine. I forced the issue to prove it, and the result was clear. I was his father."

He kissed my hand, then released it and stood, pacing. "Every year, I send him a birthday card. I write him all the time and send pictures, but the letters come back unopened. The cards are returned. I have her cell number and I still call, but my messages aren't returned. The only time I hear from her is if my child support is a day late. Which I do sometimes so her lawyer has to call me. Then I get a bad picture of my son and a brief update. That's the only contact I have."

"You must miss him."

He met my eyes. "Every day. I think about him all the time. Wonder how he's doing, what he's taking in school. If he ever thinks about me."

"Is she still married?"

"Not that I know. Last time I had that sort of info, she was on her third husband. The second one petitioned to adopt Josh, and I fought that and won. But I still don't get to see him. I flew out once to Saskatchewan, and he refused to see me. I hung around for a week, showing up every day, asking for five minutes, and got nowhere.

Roxanne told me I was upsetting him, so I left. I hated the thought that my presence was hurting him." He tugged on his hair, clearly emotional and upset. "She got some sort of restraining order against me, saying I was harassing her and Josh. Then she moved again, and I have no idea where. All my contact is through her lawyer. My last three calls weren't even acknowledged. My lawyer said there was nothing he could do for me, so I have been trying to figure things out on my own. And failing badly," he admitted with a frown.

Unable to bear his pain or the distance, I went to him, wrapping my arms around his torso. "I'm so sorry, Dom. If I'd had any idea, I would never have brought out—"

He shook his head, silencing me. "You didn't know. No one does."

"Why don't you talk about him?"

"It hurts too much. And I'm ashamed. Sometimes I wonder if I should have fought harder, played dirty the way she did."

"It sounds as if you tried to put him first. It also sounds as if you keep trying."

"My father walked out on me when I was six. I didn't want Josh to think I abandoned him. I know that hollow feeling it leaves in your life."

"Do you think your ex poisoned him against you?"

He nodded. "She was great at manipulation. Always the victim." He barked out a humorless laugh. "I was always the villain. Even when we were together. She even had me believing I was a bad guy at one point." He rested his chin on my head, his voice low. "Sometimes I wonder if it wouldn't have been easier to have walked away when she was pregnant. Then I remember what it felt like when he said 'Da-Da' the first time, and I know I wouldn't give that up, in spite of the pain I feel all the time." He swallowed. "I miss him every day."

"I understand. I almost lost Hannah, and if I had, I would have been grateful for the years we had together."

He pulled back. "Lost her? How?"

"She was shot on the job. They weren't sure she was going to pull through," I said, my voice quavering as the memory of that awful time went through my mind. "Her partner died."

He cupped my face. "Jesus, baby, I didn't know."

"That's why she left Toronto. Went to Lomand. It was smaller, safer."

"But you miss her."

I nodded. "But knowing she is happy and safe is more important than her being here where I would worry myself sick daily."

"That's how I feel about Josh. He's safe. In the pictures, he looks happy. I have to be satisfied with that. Hope that one day he reaches out and lets me tell my side of the story. Allows me to get to know him."

"I hope that happens for you," I whisper. "He should know what a great guy his father is. That you put him first, despite the pain it caused you."

"You understand."

"Yes," I agreed. "I do." A realization hit me. "That's why you let people think you're a love-'em-and-leave-'em type. It's all a front."

"Yes. I didn't want to fall for someone again and lose them. I didn't get close to anyone after I lost Josh." He smiled sadly. "Until I met you. You blew all that out of the water, Cherry G."

Our gazes locked. "You're amazing."

He bent, brushing his mouth over mine. I rose up on my tiptoes, kissing him back. He pulled me close, deepening the kiss. There was shared pain in our caress. An understanding between us of loss and comfort. He tugged me closer, his hands slipping under my sweatshirt, tracing delicate lines of pleasure up and down my back.

"I need you," he murmured against my neck. "Please let me have you."

"I need you too," I replied, shocked at how badly I wanted him. How much I wanted to help him forget his pain. Remind him of the joy in life. In being with me. Right now. I stepped back, taking his hand and leading him to the bedroom.

I fisted his shirt, and he yanked it off, tossing it to the floor, uncaring. We kissed as I fumbled with his belt, long out of practice. He laughed low, helping me. Tugging on my leggings and pulling my shirt over my head, then staring at me as he smoothed my hair away from my face. "You are so beautiful, Cherry. Incredibly so."

I ran my fingers over the tattoo on his chest, understanding the fractured heart and date etched in his skin. I hadn't asked him about it when I first saw it, somehow knowing it was personal and painful. I pressed my lips to the poignant reminder he carried on his skin right over his own heart, and he sighed, his body shuddering as I cupped him.

"Show me," I whispered. "Forget everything but me. Us."

In seconds, I was on my bed, him looming over me. He kissed me slowly. Leisurely. Long, drugging kisses that stole my senses and made me dizzy. He lapped and nipped at my neck. Sucked and licked his way down my body, exploring every inch. Making me wild with desire. When his mouth closed around my clit, I arched off the bed, crying his name. Mere moments passed before I was coming, my body exploding into shards of pleasure.

Everything around me shimmered in light as I succumbed to the ecstasy of his mouth.

Before I could recover, he rose on his haunches, dragging me up his thighs and sliding into me. I gasped as he filled me, still adjusting to his girth. He groaned, his head falling back as he gripped my hips, pinning me in place as he moved. Every thrust brushed up against my already sensitive clit, and I whimpered as I felt the stirrings of another orgasm begin to form.

"No," I breathed out. "I can't."

Dom shifted, towering over me, my legs resting on his shoulders, sinking even deeper. "You can, and you will," he murmured, his voice low and full of dark promise. "I'm not coming until you do again, Cherry. So, let go."

I clutched the sheets, the pleasure building to an almost painful point. My body shivered and shuddered. My nipples were stiff points, my core on fire. I felt frenzied and hot. Needy and wanting. Desire peaked, the emptiness I carried within me all the time disappearing as Dom filled me. There was no room for anything but him. Us. This passion.

He lifted me higher, his fingers digging into my hips so hard, I knew they'd leave bruises. I didn't care. I wanted those marks. I wanted to look at them and remember this moment. He moved faster, grunting and cursing, the sweat on his skin glistening in the low light. "Come with me, Cherry. *Come now*," he pleaded, hitting a spot so deep, it sent me over the cliff. I cried out, my muscles clamping down, pulling him in deeper.

The world around me shattered. Splintered into thousands of shards like a mirror being hit by a brick. Lights danced behind my eyes. Colors I had never seen erupted, bright and beautiful. My body took on a mind of its own, stretching, grasping, holding him.

He yelled my name. Shouted out in pleasure. Groaned in desire. Praised me.

"That's my good girl."

"Yes, strangle my cock. Fuck. Yes."

"Like that. Yes…*yes*…*yes*!" he roared.

And then the world stood still. Our bodies peaked, slowed, then stopped. He heaved a long sigh, dropping his head to his chest. I collapsed on the mattress, boneless, spineless, unable to form words or thoughts. He kissed one ankle, then the other, loosening my legs from his shoulders. Pulling out of me, leaving me aching and empty for him. He stretched out beside me, dropping an arm over my torso, and for a few moments, there was no sound aside from our breathing.

Then he spoke, his voice gravelly and low.

"Holy shit."

I started to giggle at his words. He began to laugh, his amusement muffled in the pillow. My giggles turned into guffaws, and he rolled, tugging me close.

"I should be insulted that you're laughing after my efforts."

"I'm not laughing at your efforts," I assured him. "I'm laughing at your observation of your efforts. Short but completely accurate."

He started to laugh again. "I think I might have short-circuited my brain. That last orgasm was pretty intense."

"All of mine were," I mused.

He rose up on his elbow. "*All* of them? As in, more than two?"

"Maybe."

He grinned. "Then I did my job." He bent and kissed me softly. "As did you. Thank you, Cherry G. You were exactly what I needed today."

I smiled, running my hand through his hair. "You're welcome."

"Now, how about some cake?"

I frowned. "Are you sure?"

"Yes. Celebrate this day with me. Maybe one day, I can introduce you to Josh."

"I'd like that."

He bent and kissed me again. "So would I."

# CHAPTER EIGHT

## Dom

"Hey, you okay?" Chase asked the next day with a frown. "You've been quiet all day."

"I'm good. I've got a lot on my mind."

"Come on. Charly's got lunch. She's serving it outside."

"I'm working on this—"

He waved his hand, cutting me off. "Everyone's taking their turn. It's ours now. The office is covered, and the customer isn't coming to pick up their truck until tomorrow."

With a sigh, I set down my tools, wiping my hands. I knew when to give up on an argument. I had been so lost in thought, I hadn't even noticed others leaving to eat.

I followed Chase outside, sitting at the picnic table. Charly had outdone herself, as usual. Burgers and sausages from the grill tempted me. A huge pasta salad looked incredible.

"Special occasion?" I asked as I dug in.

Charly smiled. "Not really. I felt like cooking."

Beside her, Maxx grunted. "She does this at times. It's

a wonder I don't look like a whale the way she cooks." He chuckled. "When she was pregnant, it was constant."

"It's called nesting," I muttered. Roxanne had been that way for about a month. She'd been calm, happy, and we got along. It hadn't lasted, and I had missed it once she stopped.

Maxx chuckled, wiped his mouth, and pressed a kiss to Charly's head. "I liked it. But then again, I liked all the stages except the morning sickness."

I nodded in agreement. It had been brief but violent for Roxanne. She'd been ill twenty-four hours a day for weeks. I did all I could to help her, but I tried to stay out of the way. She'd hated me more than usual during that time. I far preferred the nesting phase.

"Yeah, that isn't a fun part of pregnancy. For mother or father."

Dead silence followed my words, and I realized I had spoken out loud.

I looked up, meeting their curious gazes. It was Charly's gentle question that broke my decision to never talk about Josh.

"You know from experience, don't you?"

I gave them the CliffsNotes of what I had told Cherry. Shared what I felt comfortable telling them. Maxx and Chase listened, Charly grabbed my hand, helping anchor me. When I mentioned Josh's birthday yesterday, her grip tightened and tears filled her eyes.

"Oh, Dom," she whispered.

Maxx moved closer to her, tucking her into his side.

"Don't cry, Charly," I begged. "I'm okay. I miss him like crazy, but I hold on to the fact that he seems happy."

"I can't imagine not seeing my children," she said.

"I had no choice."

"I know."

Stefano had joined us as I talked, and he shook his head. "You've never said a thing."

"It hurt too much. But Cherry told me I should talk about him."

Charly perked up. "Cherry? Cherry knows?"

"I was with her last night and told her. She thinks I should be more open and share with people I care about."

When I'd woken up that morning, I'd been draped across her, one hand fisted in her hair, my feet hanging over the side of her smaller bed. She'd been stroking her fingers through my hair, her touch gentle and soothing. Her voice had been quiet when she spoke.

*"You need to tell people about your son. Share him and the memories."*

And looking around at the understanding and compassionate gazes, I realized she had been right.

Charly grinned. "That's good, Dom. I'm happy for you. And we're always here for you."

"Thanks, Charly."

She squeezed my hand. "That's what friends are for."

Later that night, I was restless. Not hungry, I skipped dinner. Paced around the house. Went for a walk. Checked the local listings for places for sale. I even arranged for a couple of viewings. But I was still edgy. Finally, I realized what I wanted.

Cherry.

I wanted the comfort of her closeness. Her soft voice.

I grabbed my keys and threw open my door, stopping in shock.

Standing on my doorstep, her hand raised as if to knock, stood Cherry Gallagher.

"Cherry?" I said, dumbfounded.

"Is this a bad time?" she asked, clearly nervous.

I pulled her to my chest, kissing her like I was a starving man and she was an all-you-can-eat Vegas buffet. She flung her arms around my neck, kissing me back.

I dragged her inside, holding her tight.

"This is the best surprise in the history of surprises," I murmured. The fact that she'd come to me was incredible. Not a call, not a text.

*She was here.*

She smiled at me, cupping my face. "Yeah?"

I kissed her again. "Yeah."

I tugged her to the sofa, sitting beside her. "Did you come to see Hannah too?"

"No. Just you. I-I wanted to see you."

I bent and brushed my mouth over hers. "Thanks, Cherry G. That means more than I can say."

She grasped my hand, and I felt a tremor go through her.

"Hey, what's the matter?"

"I have something to say. If you're angry, I understand. If you want nothing to do with it, I won't be upset. But I had to come and ask."

"Baby, I doubt you could make me angry. Just tell me."

She drew in a deep breath. "I was thinking about you this morning."

Teasingly, I dropped a kiss to her knuckles. "I like the sound of that."

She huffed. "Listen to me, Mr. Salvatore."

I chuckled. "Okay, I'll behave."

"I was working on a client, and she noticed I was distracted. Now, she is more than a client, she's a friend. I should say that."

"Okay."

"We had coffee, and I told her about you."

"What about me?"

"That we were, ah, seeing each other." She took another deep breath. "And about Josh."

"Why would you bring him up?"

"Because her husband—um, I cut his hair too on occasion. He…he's a big shot lawyer. He specializes in family law. Advocating for the father whenever he can."

I blinked.

"And I thought maybe you could talk to him. Tell him your story. He might be able to help. Fiona thought so."

"Fiona?"

"His wife."

"And his name?"

"Halton. Halton Smithers."

I had heard that name. Seen it in the papers and on the news. I knew he was a heavy hitter in family law. And way above my budget.

"Fiona spoke with him. He agreed to meet with you— if you want that. A free consultation."

I blinked. A free consultation. I might not be able to afford his fees, but he might be able to give me some advice. A tip or two on how to proceed.

It was a chance.

"Are you angry with me?" Cherry asked quietly.

I turned to her, taking her hands. "How could I be angry? You wanted to help. A meeting with him could at least point me in the right direction. Maybe he'd have an idea my lawyer didn't." I grimaced. "He wasn't the best, but he was what I could afford. Roxanne wiped me out, for the most part."

"He's a wonderful man. I like him a lot. And Fiona is great. She helps him. They offered to get you in on Friday at six if you could."

"Six?"

She smiled. "I think they are extending their hours for you."

"Will you come with me?"

"Yes."

"Then set it up."

"Okay."

I sat back, watching as she sent off a text. A few moments later, she looked up. "Fiona said to bring everything you have. Halton wants to look it over. If there is any chance he could get it ahead of time, it would help."

"I could take it in tomorrow. It's all in a file box. I keep it up-to-date."

"I could drop it off to them. Save you a trip. Then when you meet with him, he'll be ready."

I stroked her cheek. "Thanks, Cherry G."

She smiled. "You're welcome."

"Stay," I asked.

"What?"

"Stay here with me tonight. Please. I don't want to be alone. I was on my way to you when you arrived."

"You were?"

I nodded. "All I could think about was you. Your presence. How much calmer I feel when you're around."

She looked pleased. "Then how can I say no?" She looked down. "I don't have anything—"

"I'll give you something to wear. I have extra toothbrushes. None of your fancy girl face stuff, but I have soap."

She laughed. "I'll make do." Then she stood. "Did you eat?"

"No."

"Me either." She held out her hand. "How about a burger at Zeke's?"

I let her pull me from the sofa. "Sounds good."

We walked to Zeke's, enjoyed a burger, not talking much, but I felt more relaxed than I had all day. I told her about sharing my story with Charly, Maxx, Chase, and Stefano and their reaction. She'd been pleased I had done so.

"They're your friends, Dom. Of course they would understand and want to be there for you."

"I guess I'm not used to that."

"You must have other friends who care about you."

"I do. But since Roxanne and Josh, I tend to hold myself back a bit. I have lots of acquaintances. People I'm friendly with. But I don't let them in."

"But I see how you give of yourself in a friendship."

I chewed my burger, thinking. "This crew is different. They're a family, and they brought me into their fold." I met her eyes. "And you blew my doors wide open, Cherry G. You make me want to stay. Be part of that family—as long as you're there with me."

Her eyes widened, and her smile broke out. It was my favorite of all her smiles. Wide, happy, and a little shy. Pleased. Her eyes crinkled, and a little dimple appeared by the left one. Tiny, hardly noticeable unless you were looking.

And I was always looking.

"I want that."

"Good."

We walked home, enjoying the fresh air and empty streets.

"It's so nice here," she observed. "So much quieter than Toronto. Even at night, I hear traffic."

"You ever thought of leaving Toronto?"

"That's where my job is."

"People in Lomand and other little towns have hair too."

She laughed. "It's harder to find a job at my age. They want younger, less-experienced staff to train. I have thought about it—I even looked into getting a job closer to Hannah. So far, no luck." She sighed. "And I'll admit, there are times I wonder if I should do something else. It gets harder to be on my feet all day. And my shoulders and hands ache more than they used to."

"What would you do?" I asked, curious.

She shrugged. "I ran my own business. I know paperwork, inventory, all sorts of things. I could manage an office, work for a business, do bookkeeping or other things. But again, no one is hiring people my age." She stopped. "Oh, look at that pretty house!"

I followed her gaze to the two-story house. Large and rambling, it had ivy growing up one side and a large bay window. A fence surrounded the huge yard, and it had a double-car garage.

"Nice," I agreed, studying the lines.

"It's the sort of house I used to dream of," she mused. "Not many like that in Toronto unless you're a millionaire."

"You want a house?"

She shrugged. "I can't afford one. And I wouldn't want all that space on my own. I would love a garden and a porch to sit on, but I can come and live vicariously through Hannah."

I smiled and stored that little bit of information away for later. I kept lots of tidbits about Cherry G in my head.

We kept walking, arriving back to my house in a short time. She changed into a T-shirt and shorts I gave her, both too big but looking adorable on her. I turned on the TV, loving how she snuggled beside me on the sofa while we watched the news and caught up on the world. It felt natural to have her with me. After a while, she fell quiet, and her head became heavier on my shoulder. I glanced down, seeing that she had fallen asleep. I wasn't surprised. She'd worked all day, driven here to see me, and I had kept her up late last night and woken her once in the dark to have her again. She had to be tired.

I shut off the TV and carefully maneuvered her into my arms, carrying her to the bed. I slid her under the blanket and joined her a few moments later. She nestled against me with a sigh, and I relaxed beside her, amazed at how much I liked having her there. Her soft presence was a balm to my soul. I had never experienced such a contented feeling as I did from simply having someone this close.

But then again, I had never met Cherry G before.

I pressed a gentle kiss to her forehead and closed my eyes, letting sleep find me.

With her there, it came quickly.

I woke in the morning with Cherry curled around me, her head on my chest. I carefully pushed her hair off her face, studying her in the early morning light. Her long lashes rested on her cheeks, and her lips pursed as she slumbered. I loved the freckles on her skin—they were lighter than Hannah's and mostly scattered across the bridge of her nose and over the tops of her cheeks. I thought they were sexy and alluring. She'd informed me they were a pain in her butt when I had expressed my opinion. At the moment, with her still asleep, they were charming and sweet. Much like she was. Quiet, still, and not telling me off or flipping her gorgeous hair at me—all actions that I actually loved. Her spunk was a turn-on for me.

I glanced at the clock and then regretfully pressed a kiss to her forehead. "Hey, sleepyhead, time to wake up."

She frowned, stretching her toes and shivering, then burrowing back into me. "No," she muttered. "Not yet."

"Baby, it's seven. I know you have to drive in this morning, and I want to have breakfast with you first."

She huffed a little sigh of air and opened her beautiful eyes, meeting my gaze. "Breakfast? As in coffee?"

I chuckled. "Coffee and a breakfast sandwich if you let me up."

She looked around. "How did we get in the bed?"

"You fell asleep, and I carried you."

"You didn't wake me up to, ah…" She trailed off.

I stroked her warm cheek. "You were tired. So was I. I wanted to stay close. It's not all about sex for me, you know."

"Oh."

"Sleeping beside you makes me exceedingly happy."

"Oh," she repeated.

I gripped the back of her neck. "And horny, but that is beside the point."

She slid her hand under the blanket, stroking my morning wood. "Maybe we have time for you to make your point."

I groaned at the feeling of her hand on me. "You might be late."

"My first appointment is at ten."

"I'm supposed to be at the garage at eight."

"Oh well."

I rolled her over. "I'm about to be late, and you're about to be very noisy."

"Is that right?"

I grinned down at her. "Guaranteed."

"Prove it," she whispered.

And I did.

Twice.

# CHAPTER NINE

## Dom

I drove into Toronto Friday afternoon, my stomach in knots, my grip on my steering wheel too tight. Part of me dreaded this meeting, hearing Halton Smithers tell me there was nothing I could do and I needed to move on. I was sure I would never move on from trying to see my son. I hoped Halton would at least give me the name of another lawyer I could use. A way to fight the restraining order and get a chance to see my son.

I parked behind Cherry's building and walked into the salon. She was cleaning up, and she met my gaze with a soft smile. She walked to me, her dress swirling around her calves. The deep green set off her coloring, and her hair was swept off her face in a loose knot, tendrils dancing around her face and neck.

"You look so handsome," she whispered, rising up on her toes to press a kiss to my mouth.

I glanced down. I wanted to make a good first impression. I had showered and changed from my usual jeans and T-shirt. I had swapped out dark dress pants and a button-down shirt. Loafers. I didn't go so far as a tie. I hated those things and only wore one when necessary.

"Thanks," I replied. "You look beautiful." I offered her a tight smile, my nerves stretched to the limit.

She cupped my face. "It's going to be fine," she assured me. "Halton is going to help. I can feel it."

I squeezed her hand. "I'm afraid to hope."

"I know. But I'll be right beside you."

I touched her cheek with our clasped hands. "That's why I can do this, Cherry G."

"I'll get my purse."

"Okay."

Halton's law office was large. Impressive. His assistant Rene escorted us to the boardroom. Halton's wife, Fiona, came in to say hello. She was a pretty woman with startling silver-white hair, considering her age. She shook my hand, her warmth and friendliness evident.

"Cherry G tells me you work here with your husband."

She laughed, the sound pleasant. "Cherry G. I love that. I help Halton and Rene out. I work for BAM part time and here on occasion." She rubbed her baby bump. "When I'm not busy baking another baby for Halton to spoil."

Cherry laughed with her. "Remind me when you're due?"

"Not for another eight weeks. I swear I get bigger every time." She smiled at me. "This is number three."

"Congratulations."

"Thank you. Now, can I get you some coffee? Water?" She paused. "Scotch?"

"I'll take one of each." Halton Smithers walked in,

stopping beside his wife. He pressed a kiss to her head. "But Rene will fetch them. You get off your feet."

We shook hands, each sizing the other up. Halton Smithers was tall with broad shoulders. I was certain his suit cost more than my rent for six months, and he wore it well. His hair gleamed under the lights, and his dark-blue eyes were intelligent and shrewd. But kind. He greeted Cherry with a kiss on the cheek and indicated for us to sit at the large table.

"If you don't mind, I'd like Fiona to sit in with us. She's been helping me investigate. She's bound by the same confidentiality as I am."

"I have no problem with that." Cherry trusted her and Halton, so I did as well.

Rene came in, carrying a tray. Water, coffee, and even the scotch and glasses were on it. He slid it on the table and left, returning right away with a tray of sandwiches. "In case anyone is hungry." He eyed Fiona with a knowing look. She grinned at him then looked my way.

"I'm always hungry these days."

Cherry smiled in amusement. "I remember that stage."

Halton pushed the tray toward his wife. "Eat," he said, his adoration evident in his voice. "Please help yourself. I know it's dinnertime, so I think we can all have a sandwich and take a moment to get to know one another."

I accepted a cup of coffee but refused a sandwich. I eyed the scotch but decided to wait. I needed a clear head. Halton wolfed down two sandwiches quickly, offering a rueful laugh. "I was in court this afternoon. No lunch."

He poured a cup of coffee, then a finger of scotch into two glasses, pushing one my way. "You look as if you need this, Dominic."

"Dom."

He nodded. "Dom, it is." He tapped the familiar box

Rene had carried in a few moments ago. "First off, let me say, I wish all my clients were as meticulous as you are in keeping records. It was easy to go through and gave me exactly what I needed to know and determine the best course of action."

"Is there a course?" I asked, grateful when Cherry intertwined our fingers.

"There is." He paused and drained his coffee. "I'm a blunt man, Dom. I speak my mind, and I don't say things I don't mean. You okay with that?"

"Absolutely. I prefer blunt."

"Good." He indicated the box with a tilt of his head. "You were fucked over. Your lawyer had no clue what he was doing. And I'm not surprised you lost so often."

I drew in a painful breath. "He was recommended to me. I thought he tried hard."

"Oh, he did. But he was up against one of the worst lawyers around. Your ex-wife's lawyer is a slimy lowlife and barely operates within the boundaries of the law. He fights dirty and encourages his clients to do so as well. They tag-teamed really well. Your guy was no match for their manipulation."

I sat back, shocked. "So, I'm fucked."

Halton shook his head. "You *were* fucked," he said slowly. "But you have me now." He rapped on the table. "I'm going to help you get your son back in your life."

For a moment, I was sure I had heard him wrong. I stared at him, then looked at Cherry. She squeezed my hand.

"I'm sorry, what did you say?"

Halton smiled in understanding. "I went through your files, Dom. Got Fee to start digging. Rene, too. You were screwed over. You're still being screwed over. I'm going to put a stop to it. I'm going to find a way to let you see your son."

"I don't even know where he is," I said, disbelieving.

"He's in Kingston."

I blinked. "Kingston? As in, an hour away from me?"

"Yes."

"How did you find him?"

"Your ex is lazy, and so is her lawyer. The payments you send are deposited into her bank account. It wasn't hard to use my, ah, resources to find where they were deposited and the information linked to the account." He shook his head. "Her lawyer should have deposited the funds on her behalf and transferred the payments. But as I said, lazy."

I couldn't believe Josh was so close. I could have passed him on the street and not known it.

"You did nothing wrong. You put your son and his needs above everything. Your ex is carrying out a personal vendetta that has hurt both you and Josh," Halton said, his voice kind. "I would like to put a stop to that."

I leaned forward, feeling desperate. "Please take my case. I was saving for a house, but I'll use that for your retainer. I just want to see my son," I begged. "Talk to him. Hug him. Take him out for pizza. I'm not trying to steal him from his mother. I want to be a part of his life. I'll do anything, Halton. I'll figure out a way to pay your fees. I'll—"

He held up his hand, silencing me and shaking his head. "Everyone needs a home, Dom. A place to belong." He looked between Cherry and me. "Someone to share it with and make life wonderful. Don't use your savings to pay me." He shared a glance with Fiona, and another tender smile passed between them. He sat back, threading his fingers together and placing his hands across his chest as he regarded me.

Before I could say anything else, he spoke again.

"The laws and the courts still favor the mother, although things have come a long way. In many cases, that *is* what is best for the child. In some, it isn't. There are fathers desperate to be part of their kids' lives. Willing to do almost anything to be with them. Usually, it's an issue between the parents, as in your case. A personal grudge." He paused and rubbed his chin. "Often spouses punish each other, but it's the kids who suffer. On Saturdays, I work with a group of dads like yourself. Wanting to be with their kids, struggling to find a way to do so. You should come with me. Sit and talk to these men who understand your pain and frustration. I offer guidance, help them navigate the system. On occasion, I represent one. And a few times a year, when a case touches me, I take it on fully —pro bono." He met my gaze, his determined and serious. "Yours slammed into my heart, Dom. I want to help you reconnect with your son. If you trust me enough to allow me to take it on, I will do everything in my power to make that happen. I can't guarantee you results, but I will bloody well try."

"You'll take it on," I repeated slowly, unsure I had heard him correctly.

"I'm taking your case on pro bono. I'll work with you. You'll have the power of my office behind you, and we will do everything we can to get you back to Josh."

I sat back in shock. Turned my head and looked at Cherry. Her eyes were wide and filled with tears. She met my gaze, grabbing my hand. I realized I was shaking.

"Are you serious?" I managed to get out.

"As a heart attack. I need some time to go through everything carefully. Formulate a plan. Mount a case and refile your request for visitation—to start. Josh is older now, and he has a say in this as well. I hope he wants to see you too."

"It's been so long—"

He shook his head. "Kids have memories too." He tapped the box. "Inside here is every card and letter you tried to send to him. Years of letters, birthday cards, Christmas cards. All dated and stamped, proving how hard you tried. Letters to Roxanne. These prove you didn't give up. And I'm not going to give up until the day I see you hug your son."

I stared at him in disbelief.

"How do you feel?" he asked.

"Scared," I admitted.

"Why?"

"Because you're making me hope, Halton."

He smiled. "Hope is good, Dom. Hope is good."

Cherry led me across the street to a bar Halton and Fiona told her had good food. I was barely able to walk, never mind converse. We entered the bar, and she tugged me to a booth, ordering us drinks and burgers. Then she sat quietly, letting me process.

"How are you feeling?" she asked when I finally reached for the Guinness she had ordered me.

I took a sip, thinking. Halton had told me to be patient. He'd scheduled another meeting in two weeks and, in the meantime, gave me the information on the group he met with on the weekends. Then he told me to go and eat something, think it over, and email him any questions. He made sure I had his cell number. He shook my hand, and Fiona hugged me goodbye. It was all I could do to mumble my thanks. Follow Cherry where she led me.

"Overwhelmed."

"I can see that."

I leaned forward, resting my elbows on the table between us. I reached for her hands, holding them tight. "Grateful."

She nodded. "Halton is going to help you."

"I know that. But I meant you, Cherry G. I'm grateful for you. This is happening because of you."

"I just asked a friend."

"Your question has probably changed my life. I have a chance now. A chance to see Josh. To reestablish a relationship with my son." I squeezed her hands. "Because you asked."

Our burgers came, and she smiled. "Please eat."

They smelled great, and I hadn't eaten all day. Suddenly, I was starving, and I picked up the thick sandwich, taking a bite. We were mostly quiet as we ate, making a few observations about the bar and the food. After, we sat finishing our drinks, and Cherry met my eyes and asked the million-dollar question.

"What if Josh doesn't want to see you?"

"I thought of that. It would gut me, but I wouldn't stop. I would let him know my door was always open. I would ask to be informed of his big moments. Graduation, that sort of thing, so I could go and be there—even if he didn't want to talk to me. Maybe one day, he'd change his mind, and I'd want him to know I never gave up."

"I think he is lucky to have you for his dad."

"I think I'm lucky to have you in my life." I tilted my head to the side. "You are in my life, right, Cherry G?"

"As long as you behave," she replied tartly, tossing her head, the tendrils around her face moving.

"I can't guarantee that."

"I probably need to stick around to make sure," she countered. "Someone has to."

Suddenly, I needed her alone. I stood and slid beside her, pulling her into my arms. I kissed her deeply, holding her tight. "I'm taking you home now, pretty lady. I need to be alone with you." I kissed her again. "And I won't be behaving. Neither will you."

"Good to know."

"I'll get the check."

# CHAPTER TEN

## Dom

The next two weeks passed slowly. Waiting was nothing new to me. Time in the world of legal affairs was different from real time. A minute meant a day. A little while could be weeks. The wheels of justice were slow to move. I knew Halton needed time to prepare. To determine the best course of action. To file the right papers. It was all I could do not to call him daily and ask if I could do anything to help. I knew I couldn't—that was why he was taking over.

I worked, helped Chase with his roof and deck. I saw Cherry whenever I could, often driving to spend time with her in the evenings. I loved it when she came to visit Hannah and I got to have her with me at night. We were getting closer, and I loved spending time with her. She was every bit as stubborn and willful as ever, pushing back when I got, as she declared, "too bossy," but I did love her fire.

I also loved the soft, sweet side of her. Waking up next to her and seeing her sleepy smile in the morning. The welcoming light in her eyes as I would close the distance between us and make love to her. She was addictive, and I found I missed her on the mornings when I woke up alone. My bed felt empty. A day wasn't complete unless I talked to her. Shared part of my day with her. Listened to her voice telling me an amusing story about the girls in the salon or a funny customer.

I pulled up in front of the building where Halton was having his group meeting today to help dads like me. I felt nervous, wiping my hands down my jean-covered legs as I headed to the door. I wasn't used to talking about Josh. Sharing my story. I always had a feeling of shame—as if I hadn't done enough. Halton assured me I needed to hear other stories and realize how much I had in common with other men who found themselves in the same boat.

*"You're not as alone as you think you are in this situation,"* he *assured me.*

"Dom?"

I stopped walking, turning to face the voice, shocked to see Cherry waiting by the door.

"Cherry G?" I asked, confused.

She stepped forward, looking nervous. "Fiona called me and said Halton thought you might need a little support today. I, ah, took the day off. But if you don't want—"

I cut her off, dragging her into my arms and kissing her. "I want," I insisted. "Thank you."

She smiled up at me. "Good. I want to be here for you."

Footsteps behind us made me look up. Halton and Fiona were coming toward us, both smiling.

"Ah, the cavalry," Halton said with a wink. "I thought you might need your own backup."

"I was confused since I thought it was dads only," Cherry admitted.

Halton shook his head. "Fee comes with me a lot. The men love her. I have a feeling they'll love Cherry too. You ladies can offer insights I cannot, and frankly, you are both a lot prettier than the ugly mugs I have to stare at around the circle." He laughed with a wink. "Present company excluded, of course."

He held open the door. "Ready?"

I took a deep breath, holding Cherry's hand tightly. "I guess so."

Two hours later, I sat across from Halton and Fee, sipping a cup of coffee and eating a sandwich. The group had been enlightening. I was shocked to hear the same stories play out over and over. Men like me, who wanted to be part of their children's lives and were shut down at every turn. Listening to their pain reflected in their voices was an eye-opener. They felt the same way I did. The worry and fear they weren't doing enough, yet trying every possibility, searching every avenue open to them. Halton sat among them, his attention focused on each man as he spoke. He offered advice, encouragement, handed out business cards of other lawyers, his own, various agencies the men could try to use. He often touched Fiona, holding her hand or resting his palm on her swollen stomach, as if needing to assure himself his child was there, safe and close. The small group of men were all friendly and cordial. They welcomed Cherry and me, and I wasn't surprised that they responded to her warmth. She was empathetic and listened to them, more than once wiping away a tear. One man, Hank, described finally getting to see his daughter after six months of fighting with lawyers and his ex.

*"Nothing can compare to the feeling of her arms around my neck*

*and hearing her call me Daddy," he said quietly. "To hold her and let her know how much I missed her." He had drawn in a deep breath. "Thanks to Halton, I got that chance, and I have managed to get visitation again. His advice and the help of a different lawyer made all the difference."*

As I had learned the hard way, the right lawyer made a huge impact. If I had a plumbing problem, I wouldn't bring in a bricklayer. Not all lawyers were one-size-fits-all.

Halton chewed the last of his sandwich, wiping his mouth and picking up his coffee. He eyed me over the rim. "So, I have some news."

I sat up straighter, my hand immediately going to Cherry's leg and gripping it.

"I have a motion to reopen your visitation." He paused. "Your ex isn't happy, but the judge we got is known for agreeing with the experts that a child should have both parents in their life. He reviewed the files I gave him and agreed to a meeting."

All at once, I felt cold and hot. Worried and excited. Scared and jubilant.

He held up his hand. "It could be supervised at first."

"I don't care. I just want to see him for myself. Talk to him. Anything. Five minutes."

Halton smiled. "I think we can do better than that. Your records and all the cards and letters you kept are the ace in the hole, Dom."

I sat back, shaking my head in disbelief. "I almost gave up. Threw them all out."

"Good thing you didn't. It shows you never stopped trying." He studied me. "You prepared for this? For what could happen?"

"I am. I've been looking at houses with Josh in mind. A room of his own in case he ever wanted it. A place for him with me."

Halton smiled. "Good goals. We'll take it a step at a time, okay? Three weeks from Tuesday until we meet. I was lucky to get a date that fast. The judge had an opening. It will be a private meeting with us and her side and the judge."

I reached across the table and shook his hand. "Thank you."

He grinned. "We're just getting started, Dom."

Halton and Fee's car disappeared around the corner, and I looked down at Cherry. "You have plans this afternoon?"

"Nope," she replied. "You are my plans."

"Come home with me. I have something to show you."

"Is that a euphemism for something?"

I laughed and bent to kiss her. "No, I actually have something to show you. I need your opinion."

"Okay. I'll follow you."

"No, drive with me. You keep me calm."

She smiled in understanding. "A lot to take in," she surmised.

"Yeah. The thought that maybe in a few weeks I could see Josh? After all this time? Unbelievable."

I held out my hand. "Please."

She linked our fingers. "Okay."

We didn't talk a lot on the drive, both of us lost in our thoughts. So many things were changing—and all of them good. I glanced over at Cherry, who was staring out the window, a soft smile on her lips.

All the good was stemming from her.

I lifted her hand and kissed it. She leaned her head back on the leather and smiled at me. "What was that for?"

"For being you. For being here with me."

"You're very sweet, Mr. Salvatore."

I chuckled. "I have my moments."

I pulled up in front of the house I'd been looking at and indicated it. "I want your opinion."

"Oh, okay."

We walked around, inspecting the little bungalow. It was small but decent. I frowned as I looked at the backyard. "Good if it were just me," I mused. "But not big enough anymore."

"I agree," Cherry said. "No space for Josh to grow or be outside."

In the car, we headed to my place, but I stopped a few blocks over. The house Cherry had admired was still for sale, and it had an open house sign out front. I looked at her. "You wanna look?"

"Oh yes," she agreed enthusiastically. "I would love to see inside."

We wandered through the house, and I watched Cherry fall in love. The hardwood floors, the wood trim, even the old-fashioned layout of it. "I love rooms," she explained. "I know open concept is popular, but a formal dining room, a separate living room? I love that."

Upstairs, the three bedrooms were a generous size. The backyard was fenced, and the double garage was in great shape with tons of room.

"Perfect for a family," the real estate agent said.

She was right. This house deserved a family. Not a single guy on his own.

Except, the niggling thought that maybe I wouldn't be on my own kept popping up in my head. Maybe Josh would be here at times.

Maybe Cherry.

Maybe the three of us together.

Cherry was examining the closet the previous owner had expanded. "Look at all this space… It's incredible!"

She loved this house. I did too.

With a start, I realized I could see her here. With me.

Not on occasion, but every single day. Living with me. Sharing my life.

Completing my life.

I wondered how she was going to feel when I told her.

I tried not to laugh. I had a feeling it was going to be fireworks.

But it was gonna happen.

I was determined.

Tuesday, I called Cherry to confirm dinner. She sounded tired when I spoke with her.

"Can I take a rain check?" she asked.

"What's wrong?"

"It's just been a day. The girls are driving me mad at the salon—they're so lazy. I've been after them all day to do their jobs. Apparently folding towels and cleaning is below them now," she huffed. "I have a headache, and I'm not in a great frame of mind. All I want is to head upstairs and have a nap and a quiet night."

I was disappointed, but I understood. "Sure, baby. No worries. I'll call you later, okay? Or you call me when you get up from your nap. If you want company, I'll drive in."

"I'm going to take a couple of Tylenol and a Gravol. The Gravol makes me sleep hard, so you might not hear from me."

I chuckled. "Okay. Just feel better."

"Thank you."

I hung up, staring at the phone. Chase came in, sitting down. "What's up?"

"Nothing. Cherry canceled tonight."

"Is she okay?"

"Yeah. Bad day."

He nodded. "She said something to Hannah on the weekend too. She thinks she's too old to be hairdressing anymore. Between the girls she's working with and standing all day, she's tired of it."

I hummed in agreement. I had rubbed her shoulders on Saturday evening, shocked at how knotted her muscles were. Her legs were tight too.

"Hard on the body after all these years, I guess." I chuckled. "I feel the same at times, bent over an engine. I can't quite stretch the same way anymore."

Chase laughed. "Old man."

I glowered at him, even though, today, he was right. I felt old.

"Any plans tonight?" I asked.

"We're going to the movies. There's a double feature of two old classics Hannah loves. She switched shifts to help out a coworker, so we thought we'd take advantage."

"Cherry saw the advertisement for that. I thought I'd take her next week. It's still playing, right?"

"Yep. Every Tuesday for a month. She'd enjoy it. They both love the old classics." He paused. "Hannah worries about her mom alone all the time." He glanced at me with a sly smile. "You plan on changing that, Dom?"

I sat back, lacing my fingers behind my head and meeting his gaze. "I might be. How do you think Hannah would feel if her mom were closer?"

"She'd love it."

"I want Cherry to move in with me. I want to buy a bigger place. Have room for her—and hopefully Josh."

"Wow."

"I know."

"How does Cherry feel about that?"

I grinned. "I haven't brought that up yet. I'm waiting for the right moment."

"The way you two spark, that should be a fun conversation."

"One I plan on winning."

He stood. "I live with her daughter. The stubbornness runs deep in those two. Good luck with that."

He left and I chuckled. I had a feeling when it came to Cherry Gallagher, I was going to need all the luck I could get.

# CHAPTER ELEVEN

## Dom

About half an hour later, I was restless. Edgy. Figuring a drive would help, I grabbed my keys. I headed toward Toronto, deciding I would check on Cherry and, if she felt better, take her out. If not, I would go across the street and bring back some soup from her local Chinese place, then tuck her in for the night. But I wanted to see her. I needed to see her. She would help ease the restlessness I was feeling.

It was overcast and misty as I drove, the weather suiting my mood. The street was mostly deserted, the rain beginning as I turned onto the street where the salon was located. The area around me was foggy, the damp of the rain all around. Down the block ahead of me, I saw a small crowd. At the same time, I smelled it.

*Smoke.*

I parked and jumped from the vehicle. The rancid smell got stronger, and I realized the fog was more than fog.

The salon was on fire.

My heart plummeted when I realized how thick the smoke was.

I raced toward the side, shouting at the crowd. "Did anyone call 9-1-1?"

A woman responded with a yes. "They're on their way." She waved toward the building. "The salon is closed."

"The apartments," I snapped. "Are the occupants out?"

"We hammered on the doors, but no one is home, thank goodness," someone else said.

Cherry's words came back to me. *The Gravol makes me sleep hard…*

She was up there. Asleep. I knew it.

I raced down the back to the steps, taking them two at a time.

I heard someone behind me. "We checked!"

"She's unconscious!" I yelled back. I didn't stop running, slamming my shoulder into her door. It took me three attempts before the wood splintered and I fell inside Cherry's small apartment. It was dark, filled with smoke.

I shouted her name, grabbing a bundle of material on the floor and covering my face. I realized it was a sweater she often wore and left by the door.

I couldn't see anything as I stood, trying to find my way through the smoke, shocked at how easy it was to get lost in the swirling fog and heat. I headed toward the bedroom, tripping over something. I fell, hitting my head, cursing. I felt the warm blood dripping down my face, but it didn't matter. Finding her mattered.

I crawled, finding my way to the bedroom, shocked to discover that she wasn't in the bed. At first, I was relieved. Maybe she had gotten out. Maybe she never made it upstairs. Then I recalled the sound of the chain breaking as the door gave way. The chain wouldn't have been on if she was out. Frantically, I began to search, ignoring the blood on my face, and the choking sound I was making from the smoke. I crawled toward the front door, my hand finding a foot to one side. Cherry was in a heap on the floor, the table beside her knocked over. Squinting, I could see that she had a gash on her head and her arm was bent at a strange angle. With a huge effort, I pulled her into my arms and stood. The smoke was pouring out the door, and I headed in the direction of the air movement, gasping for oxygen as I broke through the entranceway onto the landing outside. I carried her downstairs, fighting to breathe, desperate to help her. I laid her on the cold, damp ground, immediately beginning CPR. Her chest was barely moving as I fell into a rhythm, pumping her chest and breathing into her mouth, happy to give her what little oxygen I could.

Paramedics and firefighters rushed toward us, and one reached for her. "Let me take her, sir."

I looked down at her face. Bloodied, bruised, and marked with soot. Her chest was still barely moving.

"She's inhaled a lot of smoke," I said, shocked at the sound of my own voice. Gritty. Raspy. "Please help her."

"So have you. You both need to be looked at."

Moments later, she was on a gurney, oxygen being pumped into her as they worked on her. I sat on the tailgate breathing in the mask they insisted I put on, while another paramedic checked out my cut. "Stop fidgeting," she said. "I need to clean this gash and stop the bleeding. I'm Sheila, by the way. And you are?"

"I'm fine," I insisted. "Look after her." Then I huffed. "And I'm Dom. That is Cherry."

"Cherry is in good hands. Tom is looking after her. You

need to be looked after too," Sheila informed me. "You were very brave to go in after her. And foolish."

I shook my head, unable to take my eyes off Cherry. "She's mine. I had to."

Sheila put her hand on my arm. "She's lucky to have you."

"Is she going to be okay?" I asked, coughing.

Sheila handed me a bottle of water, which I gratefully drank. She looked at Tom, who nodded.

"She's inhaled a lot of smoke, and we think she has a concussion. Her arm is broken. But all recoverable." She glanced over her shoulder. "I can't say the same for the building."

I followed her gaze. Cherry's home and place of business were gone. She was hurt.

I shut my eyes, realizing if I hadn't decided to drive in, it could be much worse.

"I need to call her daughter."

I saw movement from the gurney, and Cherry struggled to sit up, clearly panicked and confused. I stood, dropping the mask and climbing into the rig, ignoring Tom's and Sheila's protests.

I bent over Cherry, cupping her face. She was coughing and looking around wildly.

"Cherry, baby, it's me. I've got you."

"Dom," she gasped, her voice barely audible. She wrapped her hands around my wrists.

"I got you," I repeated. "You're safe."

"I woke up… There was smoke. I couldn't find my way."

"I found you."

"Why?" she asked.

I didn't know if she was asking why I came. Why I risked my life. Why I had to find her.

I had the same reply to all the questions.

I bent and gently pressed my lips to her head.

"Because I love you."

"Dom!"

I pulled my aching head out of my hands and stood. Hannah rushed across the waiting room, Chase close behind her. Unable to get a hold of her, I had called Charly, who'd taken charge and sent Maxx to the theater to get Hannah and tell her what happened. He drove them into Toronto, making sure they arrived safely.

Hannah was visibly upset, gripping Chase's hand as she stopped in front of me.

"Your head!" she gasped.

Ignoring the pain it caused, I shrugged. "They said it was too deep for butterfly bandages. The stitches make it look worse than it is."

Hannah grabbed my arm. "I spoke with the paramedics, Dom. They said you risked your life to get her. You saved her."

I frowned. "Of course I saved her. She needed me."

Hannah flung her arm around my neck, hugging me hard. "Thank you," she whispered brokenly.

I hugged her back as best I could, considering she was still holding on to Chase with a tight grip, as if she needed him to stay standing. "She's going to be okay," I assured her. "I spoke with the doctor, and he said she has a concussion, a broken arm, some bruising, and, of course, the smoke inhalation. They're going to keep her overnight for observation."

"Her apartment?" Chase asked.

I shook my head. "Gone. All of it. And the salon."

Chase pulled Hannah close. "It's okay, Cinnamon. She'll stay with us."

"She'll stay with me," I responded, my voice firm. "I'll look after her."

They blinked at my tone, and I drew in a calming breath. "I have room. And I can adjust my shifts."

"She's my mom," Hannah protested.

"She's mine to care for."

A slow smile spread across Hannah's face. "Is that a fact, Dom?"

"Yes."

"I guess we'll see about that."

She headed to the nurses station, speaking to one of the women. She turned her head and looked at me, rolling her eyes, then headed to the back.

Chase glanced at me. "Should I ask?"

"They wouldn't give me any information or let me see her unless I was family."

"So you told them…?"

"I was her husband."

"Which makes Hannah your…"

"Stepdaughter."

"I guess that sort of makes me your son-in-law."

I rolled my eyes. "Whatever."

He grinned. "Okay then…*Dad*."

"Shut it."

"Can I have a bigger allowance?"

"Chase…" I warned.

"Maybe we can play ball on Sunday."

His teasing made me smile. "Whatever." I sat down, suddenly tired. He sat next to me.

"Seriously, you okay?"

"My head aches, and I smell like smoke. I feel as if I coughed up a lung earlier, but otherwise, I'm good." I sighed. "As long as Cherry is okay, I'm good."

"Thank you," he said quietly. "Hannah would have been devastated if—"

I held up my hand, not allowing him to finish that sentence. "Let's not go there."

"Okay. She is going to be fine. And so are you. We'll all help."

I shut my eyes, the pounding in my head becoming too much. "Good plan."

## CHERRY

The sound of Hannah's voice woke me from my dreamlike state. Or nightmare feel, if I was being honest.

Fragments floated through my brain as I struggled to open my eyes. Leaving the salon with a headache. Going upstairs and taking some medication. Lying down, then waking up confused and surrounded by fog. Except, it wasn't fog. It was smoke. Thick, rancid smoke that billowed around me, making me cough, stranding me lost in a room that a short time ago was familiar. I left my bed, falling over the rug and getting up, unsure which direction I was facing. I could see nothing but smoke. I knew I needed to move. To get to the door. But nothing seemed to work. My brain, my feet, my thought process—everything seemed to have short-circuited. I headed in what I thought was the direction of the door, except to hit the wall. I felt around, coughing and gasping for air until I felt the doorframe. I paused, drawing the map in my mind to the front door. To safety. I rushed forward, tripping over the small table, sprawling to the floor. I recalled the sharp pain in my head as well as my arm…and then nothing until I heard a voice calling my name.

Dom.

My eyes flew open, meeting Hannah's tear-filled gaze.

"Oh, Mom," she sobbed.

"Dom." I reached for her hand, my movements jerky and causing me pain. "Dom was there. Is he okay?"

She laid her hand on my cheek. "Shh. He's fine. He's outside."

"He saved me."

I knew there was another memory there, but I couldn't quite grasp it. It was something important, but my head hurt too much to concentrate.

"I know. The paramedics told me."

"There was a fire," I whispered.

She nodded. "In the salon." She met my eyes. "It's all gone, Mom. Everything."

I shut my eyes. My head hurt. My arm ached terribly. My chest felt as if someone had put a fifty-pound weight on it. My throat was scratchy. The cannulas in my nose itched, and I wanted them gone.

"Water," I begged.

A straw touched my lips, and I sipped gratefully.

"How bad?" I asked when I finished.

"You have a concussion, a broken arm, and you inhaled a lot of smoke."

The last part wasn't a surprise. I could taste the smoke. Smell it. I forced my eyes open and stared at the cast encircling my forearm.

"Pink?" I said, confused.

"I think Dom picked it." Hannah leaned forward, speaking quietly. "In order to see you, he told them you're married."

I blinked.

*"He what?"*

She smiled. "I'm gonna call him Dad and watch him freak."

"Serves him right."

Hannah gently brushed my hair off my forehead. "I think we'll cut him a little slack on this one, Mom. If it weren't for him…"

I let out a long sigh, my eyes drifting shut. I had so many questions, but I was so tired.

"When can I go home?" I managed to get out.

"Not until tomorrow. They have to watch you overnight, and you have to stay on the oxygen."

I felt the darkness pulling at me. I struggled against it, but it was stronger. A thought flitted through my mind.

"Where will I go now?" I wondered.

I felt a soft press of lips on my head. Heard the sound of another voice. One that soothed and assured. It was filled with emotion.

"You'll come with me," Dom whispered.

And I slept.

They woke me every few hours. Each time they did, Dom was there. Hannah came and went. Chase was standing beside Dom once, and he smiled reassuringly at me.

The room was lighter, my head clearer when I opened my eyes in the morning. Beside me, Dom slept, his head against the back of the chair, the bandage on his forehead bright against his olive skin and dark hair. He was in scrubs, his hair damp as if he'd showered. His long legs were crossed at the ankle, and he had one hand resting on my arm.

Beside him was a table, a jug of water beckoning. I

cleared my throat, looking for a call button, but the simple action woke him. Dom's eyes flew open, and he turned, meeting my gaze.

"There she is," he murmured, his voice rough. "Hello, Cherry G."

"Thirsty."

He poured me some water, helping me sit up, and I sipped it, grateful.

"Better?"

"Much."

He settled me back on my pillows.

"Have you been here all night?"

"Of course," he replied as if affronted I would expect him to be anywhere else.

"Your head…"

He frowned. "Is fine. The nice nurses have been looking after me. They even loaned me some scrubs and let me shower so I didn't smell like smoke as badly as I did."

"Can you convince them to do the same for me?"

He ran his finger over my cheek. "As soon as the doc checks you out."

I grabbed his hand. "You saved me."

He didn't answer.

"You saved my life, Dom. You risked your own to save me."

"I had to."

"Why?" I asked, the echo of the memory I was trying to recall last night reverberating in my mind.

He met my gaze, his eyes tired. Bloodshot. Filled with tenderness. "You know why, Cherry G."

"Please."

He leaned close. "I saved you for myself. I had to. I love you."

Hearing the words was like small explosions going off

in my head. My heart jumped, my breathing picked up, and my hand trembled as I cupped his face.

"I love you too."

It was slow to start, then it grew. Wide. Surprised. Pleased. It was a different smile than I had ever seen on his face. One I had a feeling was only for me.

"Then for the first time, we're on the same page," he said quietly.

"I think we always have been. I kinda like to argue."

He bent low, pressing his lips to mine. I was sure I reeked of smoke and my breath was equally terrible, but he didn't care. "Never change." He smiled against my mouth. "I love that stubborn part of you."

"Good."

"But you're not going to argue about the fact that I'm taking you home. With me."

"No. Hannah will look after me."

"No. I will."

"It's not your place," I argued weakly.

"I disagree."

"I don't think—"

He cut me off by placing a finger on my mouth. "I have room. Time. Hannah and Chase both work. They're young and developing a relationship."

"You work," I mumbled against his finger.

"Yep. And General Charly has it all figured out. I'm going to work scattered hours. She's going to help me. Hannah will come and look after you when she can. So will the other girls. They all want to help." He smirked. "They're already organizing meals. We both benefit, Cherry. Besides, as your husband, it's my job to look after you."

I narrowed my eyes. "We haven't discussed that lie yet."

"I wasn't staying away from you. It was either tell them

I was your husband or beat down a few security people to get to you. Either way, I was coming into the room."

Something in me melted at his possessive tone. His insistence he cared for me. I kissed the end of his finger that still touched my mouth.

"I'm going to look after you, and that is all there is to it."

"You're not the boss of me."

He hovered over me, all levity gone. "Not the boss, but the man who loves you. Who you love. I almost lost you last night, and I am not letting you out of my sight. Understand?" He swallowed. "Don't ask that of me right now."

His eyes, his words, said everything. I gave in because the bottom line was, I wanted to be with him.

"I might be a terrible patient."

A grin crossed his face, and he folded his arms, leaning on the bed. "I already know you're gonna be a handful. Ordering me around. Refusing to listen to the doctor. Trying to do too much. I can't let Hannah and Chase take that on. I can keep you in line."

I scoffed at his words, and he winked.

"I have ways, Cherry. As soon as you're feeling up to it, I'll show you all of them."

I was about to argue when I yawned, a wave of exhaustion hitting me. He kissed my hand and smiled. "Sleep, baby. I'll be here when you wake up. I'll take you home later." He paused then smiled. "Our home."

"Temporarily," I muttered.

"We'll see," he replied. "We'll see."

# CHAPTER TWELVE

## Cherry

I ached all over but insisted on a shower when I got to Dom's place. I hated the smell of smoke that clung to my skin and hair. Hannah went to the beauty supply place and got me the shampoo I asked for, and she helped me wash my hair. Even after three washings, the smoke scent was there, but at least it was more manageable. I dressed in some leggings and a loose shirt of Dom's, grateful when Hannah removed the plastic my arm was wrapped in to keep the cast dry.

"Why couldn't it be a removable cast?" I grumbled.

Dom walked in, carrying a tray. "Maybe they were fast to figure out you'd be ripping it off the first chance you got, Cherry G." He winked. "Troublemaker."

He'd showered again as well and looked more relaxed. I knew he was as tired as I felt, but not as troubled. He slid the tray onto my lap. "Lunch."

I picked up the spoon, tasting the thick soup. "Delicious."

He perched on the end of the bed. "Rosa," he said simply. "The fridge is full. Lasagna, more minestrone soup, ziti. Charly brought a couple of casseroles and did some shopping. She brought you some more clothes too." He looked upset. "All of yours are gone."

"Everything?" I asked.

He nodded. "Sorry, Cherry. Everything." He reached over and squeezed my hand. "I know how upsetting that must be."

"Not as upsetting as it would be if this had happened a month ago."

"Why?"

"When I moved in to the smaller apartment, Connie let me store a bunch of totes filled with things I didn't have room for in the apartment in the basement of the building. Not long ago, she discovered a leak, and Chase and Hannah graciously let me move them to their basement about a month ago. All my photos and a lot of my things are in those totes. The apartment was too small for me to have them out or to have too many photos around. I lost what was out, but I think Hannah has copies of a lot of the photos. The knickknacks and other things… Well, I suppose they're just things. My mother's quilt makes me sad, but…" I trailed off, trying not to cry.

"Maybe some things can be salvaged. Once we can go in, I'll pack up what we can," Dom assured me, stroking my hand.

"We'll help," Chase said, coming in with Hannah.

"Of course we will," she agreed. "If it's just smoke, we'll take it somewhere."

"We do ozone bombs in cars," Chase mused. "Gets rid of odors. Maybe we could try that on other things."

Dom nodded in agreement. "Good thinking."

"Once we can get in," I agreed, amazed at their offer. "I wonder when they'll know what it was that caused the fire."

"Soon, hopefully," Hannah murmured.

I was suddenly exhausted, and the soup no longer held much appeal. Dom looked at Hannah, who took the tray and gave it to Chase. "Sleep a bit, Mom. You might be hungrier later."

Dom helped me settle, and he gave me some pain pills. "You want me to stay?" he asked quietly.

"Yes."

Hannah smiled. "We'll come back later."

Dom walked them out and returned, pulling off the hoodie he wore, leaving him in a tight T-shirt.

"How's your head?" I asked, concerned.

"A bit touchy. I'm tired too, so a nap is a good thing. The kids are coming back later." He stretched out beside me, letting me arrange myself so I was close. I felt better when I could touch him.

I sighed quietly, hoping some sleep would help. I felt jumpy and on edge. Every time I closed my eyes, I saw the smoke around me. Felt the fear creep into my chest and make me tense. I fought back the emotion that was swelling. I was safe and here with Dom.

Yet, it kept building.

He tightened his arm around me. "You can cry, you know," he whispered, understanding my emotion. "You lost your home, your place of employment, all your things. I know you're trying to be strong for Hannah, but you don't have to pretend with me."

I looked up at him, meeting his intense, steady gaze.

"I know you're here. That I'm safe. But I feel almost… scared," I confessed. "The last time I lay down for a nap…"

"I know. I understand. You have every right to feel whatever you feel," he murmured. "But I'm right here, and I'm not going anywhere."

"If you hadn't come—" A sob escaped my mouth.

He nestled closer, pulling me to him. "I know. I keep thinking that. But I did. And you're here and safe. Nothing is going to hurt you. I promise." He pressed a kiss to my head. "Let it out, baby. You'll feel better."

I buried my face into his chest and began to cry. I let myself grieve for my lost possessions. My job. My home. How close I'd come to losing everything. Dom held me, not offering platitudes or telling me everything would be okay. He let me cry until my own thoughts changed from "what if" to "what now." I still had most of my photos and keepsakes. They were with Hannah. I never really liked the apartment, and I would find another place. I had already known I was going to have to give up hairdressing soon. My legs and shoulders couldn't do it full time anymore. I would find another job.

And I was alive. With Dom. He was with me, his heat soaking into my skin like a warm blanket. His scent wrapped around me, and the faint whiff of smoke was disbursed by his cologne. By him.

With a long shudder, my tears stopped. I wiped my face with the tissue he handed me and cuddled as close as I could get.

Then I slept.

Later, my boss called to check on me, tearfully informing me the salon was gone and she wasn't sure if she would ever reopen. I didn't tell her I wouldn't return. I wasn't ready to say that yet.

"I have no idea what happened," she wept. "The girls locked up, and they said everything seemed fine."

"Could be an electrical fire," I suggested.

"When I think of what could have happened…" she said. "I would never have forgiven myself if you had died, Cherry."

"Well, Dom got me out," I soothed.

"Thank God for that man."

I glanced over at him. He was beside me, his hand on my leg, but he was watching the news on the TV, content to be close. We both needed that right now.

"Yes," I agreed. "Thank God for that."

"I'll be in touch soon," Connie promised. "Be sure to file a claim with your insurance and get me the information."

"I will."

I sighed as I hung up the phone. "At least my car and tenant insurance are through the same company and a broker I've used for years," I said. "I know them, and they know me." I had already called my broker, and he was coming to see me and would visit the apartment site to take pictures. "I didn't have a large value for the contents since it was furnished. And what was destroyed can't be replaced," I added sadly.

Dom squeezed my leg. "Still, the claim can be filed, and you can use the money to purchase what you need. Once you find a new place." He was quiet for a moment. "Maybe this is a good time to think of relocating."

I tilted my head, studying him.

"You don't want to do hairdressing anymore. Your apartment is gone. Hannah is here." He swallowed. "So am I. Maybe you should look here."

"And do what?" I asked.

He shrugged. "You said you had experience with other things. Explore the options." He scratched the back of his neck, looking nervous. "You can stay here as long as you want. We could look for a place together."

"You want to live together?" I asked. "It's only been—"

He cut me off with a shake of his head. "I don't care if it's only been a day, Cherry G. You're it for me. I have never loved someone the way I love you. We can live together if you want that. I do. And you can take your time and find a job."

I blinked at him. He sounded so certain.

"We can look for a place together. I wanted to buy a house, so you can help me pick it. Let it be a place you love and make it our home. We can fill it with memories together. I've never had that, but I want it. I want it all with you."

Our eyes locked, and I saw it. His conviction to us, to this relationship, was clear and solid. That was what he wanted. Me. Here. With him.

"I-I have to think about it."

There was a knock on the door, and he stood, bending over me. He dropped a kiss to my mouth with a smile. "Of course you do, Cherry G. You have to think and overanalyze and worry. Wonder if you should do something that puts you first. That makes you happy. The answer to that is yes. But you do what you have to, then we'll move ahead. I'll wait." He headed to the door. "In the meantime, I'll get more places to look at."

He left me on the sofa, my mind spinning.

Everything rational and responsible told me his idea was crazy. We hadn't known each other long enough. We needed more time.

The smaller part of my brain was jumping up and down like a schoolgirl. Live with Dom. Be close to Hannah. Build a life with him. We were older, so why waste time if it felt right?

And dammit, as much as I tried to fight it, as much as I resisted, Dom Salvatore felt all sorts of right to me.

Did I dare do this?

Hannah, Chase, Maxx, and Charly came in, and I put aside my thoughts.

But that schoolgirl kept jumping.

And from the grin on Dom's face when he looked at me, he knew it.

## DOM

Cherry's gaze followed me all evening. Despite the full refrigerator, the kids had brought pizza, and we sat around, casual and comfortable, eating and laughing. But whenever I looked at Cherry, her eyes were already on me.

I knew what she was doing. Overthinking. I understood it was part of her nature. No doubt a learned habit since after her husband died, she'd had only herself to rely on, so she was careful with decisions.

I wanted her to go with her heart on this one.

In the kitchen, I stacked the dishwasher, looking up when Hannah came in, carrying some glasses. I added them to the rack, shutting the door and wiping my hands.

"What's up?" I asked, knowing she'd come in for more than assisting with cleanup.

"Mom told me what you suggested. About her moving here. Moving in with you."

I crossed my arms, leaning against the counter. "You have issues with that?"

"No. I think you're good for her."

"I sense a but."

"It's fast."

I chuckled. "Hannah, may I remind you that you and Chase went from roommates to lovers in a matter of weeks? It's the same amount of time your mom and I have been seeing each other. And frankly, at my age, I'm not the most patient of men anymore. I know what I want, and I don't want to waste months dancing around the issue." I met her gaze. "I love your mother. I want to build a life with her, and I think, despite her worries, she wants the same. I want to make her happy. She deserves that, yes?"

"Yes, she does. And I would love to have her here. And to know she isn't alone." Hannah nibbled her lip. "You really love her?"

"Absolutely."

"What about Josh?"

"I hope to get him back in my life. I think your mom would be a big part of that."

She was quiet for a moment. "I always wanted a sibling."

I chuckled. "Well, he'd be a little brother of sorts, I guess."

She grinned. "So, for sure, you'd be my step—"

I laughed, cutting her off. "If you're gonna call me Dad, then I'm going to insist on making it official with Cherry G out there." I winked. "Cherry S has a good ring to it, I think."

She blinked. "Wow. You men move fast here, don't you?"

I cocked my head to the side. "Would I have your blessing, Hannah?"

A smile curled her lips. "Yeah, Dom, you would."

I grinned. "Thanks."

I didn't say anything to Cherry. I didn't want to add to her overthinking. I wanted her to recover from what had happened so we could move forward. She was a great patient—for two days. Then she became restless and bored. She walked around the house, rearranging things. Folding and refolding blankets as best she could with one arm. Dusting things she'd already dusted. We went for walks, Hannah came and took her to lunch, but by day three, she was ready to get back to life.

We were sitting on the sofa when the call came in from her insurance adjuster. I got up to get us more coffee when I heard her gasp of anger and a string of expletives leave her mouth. My eyebrows shot up in surprise, as she rarely swore or got angry. She stood, pacing as she spoke, and I watched her, trying not to notice how sexy she was when she was mad. The color in her cheeks highlighted her prettiness, and the scowl she wore reminded me of a sexy librarian, especially given she was wearing a set of reading glasses she'd forgotten to take off.

She hung up, tossing her phone down.

"Problem, Cherry G?"

She pulled off her glasses, dropping them beside her phone. "The fire was caused by a curling iron left plugged in. It fell off the shelf onto the unfolded towels the girls never finished." She was almost growling. "It was an older one without an automatic shut off. You always check before you leave. Everything. Their carelessness cost Connie her business and me my home." She met my eyes, furious.

"It could have been worse," I reminded her.

"I know. I repeated myself over and over. They were always anxious to leave at the end of the day. I wasn't there, and they closed up without finishing their work, and now none of us has a job."

I looped my arm around her waist and pulled her close.

"I'm sorry, Cherry G. I know that must hit hard. So unavoidable."

"It makes me mad."

"I can tell. What can I do to help?"

"I know you have to go to the garage. I want to come with you. I don't want to stay here alone. I can visit Charly and the kids."

"Sure," I agreed easily. I would feel better if she was where I could see her. "You get ready."

At the garage, I got busy, fast. Cherry headed to the house, and knowing she was okay and safe, I got to work. Cars and trucks were parked everywhere, and I grabbed the schedule, figuring out my first job.

Hours later, I wiped my hands, pleased at what we had accomplished. I was headed to the staff room, needing five minutes and a cup of coffee, when I heard it. Cherry's voice and her laughter coming from the office. I walked in, surprised to see her and Charly, the computers on, invoices and inventory sheets on the desk.

"What's going on?" I asked. "This hardly looks like a visit."

Charly grinned at me. "We need help with the books and keeping up. Everyone is so busy. I hired Cherry."

I blinked. "You hired her?"

Charly looked incredibly pleased with herself. "It's perfect. She has experience and needs a job. We need help. Chase is busier than ever with his custom work. The new client is bringing more business than we thought. You're getting more in demand with your extensive experience. Cherry can take over a lot of the office stuff. She knows the software we use."

I met Cherry's gaze. Her eyes were warm and filled with excitement. She was smiling. The thought of having her here and close every day made me stupidly happy.

"Don't overdo it," I warned quietly.

"I'm not. Charly is showing me everything. I can only use the one arm, so I'll be slow, but once this silly cast comes off, look out!"

I had to grin. She had a job, which was another reason to stay here. I bent and pressed a kiss to her head. "Look out, indeed. Go get 'em, baby."

# CHAPTER THIRTEEN

## Dom

W e walked around the empty house, Cherry chewing the inside of her cheek. I felt her worries and nerves kicking into overdrive as she opened cupboard doors, peering in and shutting them, only to open the same one again.

"Cherry," I murmured. "Talk to me."

"I love this house."

"I know you do."

We were viewing the same two-story place she had loved so much. It was our third visit. Since the day she'd been to the garage, our future together seemed to be moving ahead. Getting a house together was the next step, and I knew how much she loved this one. I wanted her to have it.

"But?" I prompted as she opened the cupboard again, looking inside at the empty shelves.

"Do we need all this space?"

"I think we can fill it. Especially if Josh comes for visits. You can bring the garden back to life. Josh can kick around a soccer ball, or maybe one day, we'll add a pool."

She turned and faced me fully. "And what if nothing happens and there is no Josh?"

I blew out a hard breath. "Then it's me and you, Cherry. We can make this place ours. You'll make it our home. Josh is the cherry, but you're the whole cake and the icing. You love this place. I can afford it."

"I'll be part of the purchase. I want to share in this," she insisted.

"Fine. We'll go to the bank and do all the paperwork and buy it together. It will be ours. But you have to say yes to that…" I paused. I'd had no plans on doing this today. Here. Now. But the timing was perfect. "And you have to say yes to this." I pulled a ring from my pocket, holding it up. Cherry's eyes widened as I took her left hand in mine and slid it on, being careful not to hurt her arm. "Marry me, Cherry."

"Marry you?" she repeated.

"Yes. Hannah gave me her blessing. I want you to marry me and move in to this house with me. We'll build a life together. With each other."

"It's so fast."

I laughed. "Once you were in my heart, Cherry, it was full throttle. I know what I want, so why wait?"

She looked at her hand, flexing her fingers gingerly. The oval emerald flanked by two smaller diamonds twinkled in the light. She furrowed her brow.

"You can have it all, Cherry. Us. A home. A life here close to Hannah. Me," I added. "We can have it all together. All you have to do is say yes." I lifted her hand and kissed it. "You don't have to be alone anymore. Neither do I. Please, Cherry, marry me."

She looked up, tears glistening. "Yes."

I captured her mouth, kissing her.

"Let's make an offer."

## CHERRY

Dom's hand around mine was akin to a vise grip wrapped around my fingers. I squeezed his hand, leaning close as we waited for Halton.

"I need that hand, Dom. It's the only working one."

Instantly, he relaxed his grip. "Sorry."

I smiled at him. "It's okay. I understand."

He stroked my cheek with the back of his hand. "I know you do." He frowned, glaring at the door. "I wish you could come to this meeting."

"I know," I soothed. "But I can't. Though, I'll be waiting for you when it's done."

Halton walked through the door, his head up, shoulders back. He looked ready to fight. He stopped in front of us, shook Dom's hand, and bent, kissing my cheek. "How are you?" he asked.

"I'm fine."

"The arm giving you trouble?"

"I get an air cast tomorrow."

"Good news. I understand congratulations are in order as well."

I smiled, feeling the color creep under my skin.

Halton chuckled. "You crazy kids. I love it. A house. Engaged. Moving ahead. Perfect. It bodes well for this meeting."

"How?" Dom asked, his voice tight.

"You're settled. Getting married. Buying property. I have glowing character references from your employers, current and past. Excellent credit history. Personal references. All of this shows a stable, eager father. Judges, especially this judge, love that."

"But Cherry can't come in with me?"

"No. Roxanne can't bring in anyone but counsel either. Why don't you take Cherry to the coffee shop and get her settled, and I'll meet you up on three, okay?"

Dom huffed, and I met Halton's eyes. They were filled with understanding and determination. He lifted an eyebrow in encouragement.

"I'll be fine. I have my Kindle, and I would love a coffee. I'll be waiting."

Halton nodded. "Great."

Dom carried a tray, guiding me to the back of the crowded shop. A couple agreed to let me share their table, and he slid the tray down, helping me off with my coat. He dug out my Kindle and phone, fussing with the lid on the coffee and the package of cookies he'd insisted I needed.

I covered his hand. "I'm fine. Go upstairs and fight for your son. I'll be right here."

His shoulders dropped. "What if—"

I shook my head. "Then we'll deal with it. But Halton has this. I know it."

He lowered his head and kissed me. "I love you, Cherry. Thank you for being here."

"I wouldn't be anywhere else."

With a huff of air, he stood and headed to the door. I watched him walk away, still in awe of how he looked in a suit. The dark navy looked great on him, and although nowhere near the caliber of the suit Halton wore, it looked good, fitting Dom's broad shoulders and tapered waist well. He wore a white dress shirt and a patterned tie. He'd even pulled out a pair of dress shoes, and he looked every inch a respectable man.

A very sexy one, at that.

I couldn't begin to fathom how much my life had changed in such a short time. Only weeks ago, I was missing Hannah terribly, disliking my job and the apartment I lived in. I was always alone, unless she was visiting or I went to see her, which, given her roommate status before Chase, wasn't often. I never felt welcome at her old place. That all changed when she moved in with Chase. He'd driven into Toronto before the fire to ask for my blessing to marry her, and I was thrilled to give him my enthusiastic agreement. Last night, he'd come over to Dom's, telling me his plans on proposing on her birthday, and I eagerly offered to help. I loved him and the way he treated my daughter.

And I was going to marry Dom. Live in a house I'd fallen in love with and build new memories. No longer alone, no longer missing my daughter. Everything I loved, everyone I loved, would be close. My life had finally changed, and I could put away the sorrow I always felt and live in the present, no longer wishing for the past.

And Chase had brought a surprise with him. My mother's quilt. He and Dom had been allowed to enter the apartment briefly. Not much remained, but they got the blanket, my small jewelry box, and took the photos that hadn't been destroyed. Chase told me that Brett's girlfriend, Kelly, who was a photographer, was going to help restore the pictures when they came home from their trip. I'd lost my clothing and some items, but the quilt and the photos were worth so much more to me. The quilt had been treated and washed several times and was fine. I had been more than delighted.

"Excuse me."

I blinked as my musings were interrupted, and I looked up, seeing a woman with a young boy beside her.

"Can my son sit with you?"

I had been so deep in thought, I hadn't even noticed the couple leave the table. I was alone.

"Yours is the one table with an empty seat," the woman explained.

"Oh, sure."

"I have a meeting upstairs, and my babysitter canceled last minute," she huffed.

"I told you, I don't need a babysitter," the boy objected, color blazing on his cheeks. "I can look after myself."

"I'll watch him while I'm here," I assured her. "Happy to share my table."

She pushed him toward a chair, and he sat down heavily, rolling his eyes. I tried not to laugh. I guessed him to be about twelve, and I remembered Hannah at that age, constantly trying to prove her independence. His mother handed him a knapsack. "Your games are in there. And a snack. Get a drink if you want or something else to eat, and I'll be back as soon as I'm finished dealing with this." He nodded.

"Thank you," she added to me before hurrying away. The boy watched her, then reached into his knapsack for an iPad. He ignored me as he began to play something on it, and I sipped my coffee, opening my Kindle. I rested it on my cast that was now a little dirty and covered in drawings and funny jokes everyone at the garage had scribbled on to it. Dom wrote me love messages, and I enjoyed finding a new one from time to time.

"What did you do to your arm?"

I met the deep brown eyes of the young man across from me. His dark hair fell over his forehead, and he pushed it away impatiently, the gesture somehow familiar.

"Oh, I broke it falling over a table."

"Were you drunk?" he asked, grinning.

"No. My apartment was on fire, and I couldn't see where I was going."

His eyes became round with curiosity. "You were in a fire?"

"Yes."

"Were you scared?"

"Yes, I was. But my fiancé saved me."

"Cool."

He looked at my arm again. "What's all the writing?"

"Oh, I work at a garage, and the guys write me jokes."

"Like a mechanic shop?"

"Uh-huh," I said, taking a sip of my coffee. He reminded me of someone. The shape of his eyes and face. The way one side of his mouth lifted a little higher than the other when he grinned. He was tall and lanky. Awkward. But he seemed nice. Polite.

"I love cars. Engines."

"That's what my fiancé does."

"Wicked cool. I want to be a mechanic." Then he snorted. "My mom wants me to be something better."

"Better?"

"Someone who wears a suit and makes a ton of money."

"Ah."

"Can I see the jokes?"

"Sure."

He shut off his game and slid closer. He traced the words on my cast as he read them to himself, chuckling over a few of the silly jokes. He had long fingers, his nails ragged and uncared for. I had a feeling his mother probably nagged him about the condition a lot.

He laughed out loud at one joke, the sound so familiar,

I startled. I stared at him, then swallowed. "My name is Cherry. What's yours?"

He grinned. "Josh."

I tried to hide my shock. I was staring at Dom's son. That was the reason he looked so familiar.

This was the boy Dom was upstairs fighting for the right to get to know. To be a part of his life.

His mother had dropped him off beside me.

"How old are you, Josh?"

"Thirteen."

"Do you like school?" I asked, desperate for any information I could get to share with Dom.

"It's fine. I like science and art. Math, no."

"I like numbers."

"It's so complicated."

I pulled a pen from my purse and wrote some problems on a napkin. He frowned. "It makes no sense."

"What if you broke it down this way?" I asked.

He furrowed his brow as he looked at the numbers, tracing them the way he did with the words earlier. "Thirty-two?" he asked.

"Yes!"

"Give me another one."

Time flew by as I taught him the way my dad had taught me, breaking down the equations into parts he could understand. Replacing numbers with objects. He was smart. Funny. I asked him question after question. His favorite color. Movie. Time of day. Memory.

He paused when I asked that. He looked around as if making sure he wasn't overheard.

"I don't know if it's a memory. I'm at a park, and there's a guy. He's pushing me on the swing, then catching me on the slide. We have ice cream. It was sunny."

"Who's the guy?" I asked, my heart in my throat.

"I think it's my dad, but it's fuzzy. He left us—didn't want me or my mom. I always wondered, if he didn't want us, why he'd be so nice. So sometimes, I think it's just me thinking and wishing."

I clasped his hand. "I'm sure it's real. You know, sometimes you don't know the whole story."

He shrugged. "I guess I never will."

"Josh!" a voice called.

I looked up to see his mother striding toward us. She looked furious. "We're going. Now."

She was tall with light golden hair. Icy blue eyes. Pretty, in a hard way. Anxious to leave. She barely glanced at me. "Let's go."

"Nice to meet you, Josh."

"You too," he said. "Thanks for the math lessons."

"I hope it helps."

She tugged him away, not sparing me a glance. She pulled him through the café, disappearing through one door as Dom and Halton walked in through another one.

They came over, sitting down, and I reached for Dom's hand. "Well?" I asked, hoping how angry Josh's mom had been because things had gone well for Dom.

"I get to see him." Dom's voice was tight. "I get to see my son. I don't know if I'll even recognize him."

I leaned close. "Dom, he was here."

He gaped at me. *"What?"*

"His mom had to bring him with her. She asked if he could sit at my table. It took a few moments after she left, then I realized who he was. It was Josh."

Halton chuckled. "I told you she was your good-luck charm."

"You talked to him?"

"I did. He's so amazing."

Dom turned, gripping my hand. "Tell me everything."

Dom studied the photo I showed him, his brow furrowed. I had snapped it as Josh had lifted his head from solving a problem. He had been smiling widely, proud of himself for understanding how to use the tools I had shown him. He looked so much like his father in the photo, and I knew Dom could see that.

"This is the clearest, most up-to-date photo I have," he said thickly. "The ones I get from the lawyer are always blurry and older. He says Roxanne doesn't have a decent camera."

Halton scoffed. "She was carrying the same phone I have. Great camera. She's playing a game." He sat back, swinging his leg. "She likes games, that one. I know her type. Using the child to hurt her ex." He shook his head. "Which, in the end, hurts the child as well."

"You get to see him," I prompted. "When?"

"Next Saturday. She's bringing him to meet me at a restaurant we chose halfway for both of us at one. I get him for two hours. If he's agreeable and it goes well, I get him for the whole day the following Saturday. Then overnight the week after." Dom sighed. "I agreed to go slow so Josh isn't overwhelmed. I don't want him upset."

"And the judge saw that. He also saw through all Roxanne's objections. Her lies. Her obvious temper." Halton smirked. "When I pulled out a few of the postmarked letters you'd sent to Josh that were returned, I thought she was going to lose it. He saw that as well. It really couldn't have gone better. The fact that you kept all of it for him was huge, Dom. That you never stopped trying." He smiled kindly. "That you were still putting him first, insisting Josh have a say in this. All of that counted.

All of that *mattered*." He stood. "I'll leave you two, and I'll see you on Saturday."

"Thank you," Dom said, rising to shake his hand.

Halton shook his hand and clapped him on the arm. "This is a good win, Dom. We'll get you back in his life, and he'll be the better for it."

He bent and brushed a kiss on my cheek, whispering, "He's pretty shaken up. I'm glad he has you."

Dom sat beside me, once again picking up my phone and studying the picture. I rubbed his arm. "You okay, sweetheart?"

He smiled at my unexpected endearment. "I will be. I'm reeling, if I'm being honest."

"I can understand that."

"Halton was incredible. Precise. Authoritative. He ran over her lawyer and his underhanded manipulation like he was sipping a beer on the porch at the end of a day. Nothing fazed him. He knew what he needed to do, and he did it. I thought Roxanne was going to expire on the spot, she was so furious. He didn't let a single remark pass without refuting it. The angrier she got, the wilder her accusations became, and he squashed every single one. I wish I could have taped it."

"That must have been difficult to listen to."

"Once upon a time, yes. Today, it meant nothing. I knew I couldn't react. Halton warned me not to argue with her—to let it roll off my back. And he was right. The judge saw her temper and my calm. It was always that way, but she used to twist it around, making me sound like the crazy one." He paused. "I hope she's not done that to Josh."

"He seems great. Smart. Articulate. Curious. Funny."

"You'll come with me next week?"

"Am I allowed?"

"Yes, I specifically had Halton state I would be with my fiancée. Roxanne can't refuse."

"Then I'm there."

He leaned close and kissed me. "Thanks. Let's go home."

I gathered my purse and jacket, and we headed to the car. On the drive back to Lomand, his phone rang, and he answered on the Bluetooth.

"Dom speaking."

"Dom, it's Randy. The inspection was great. So, your offer stands. Congratulations, the house is yours."

Dom met my shocked gaze fast then returned his attention to the road. "Even with the quick closing?"

"That was perfect for them."

"Thanks, Randy. I'll be in touch later."

"Sounds good."

Dom hung up and reached for my hand. "The house is ours, Cherry."

"I can't believe we got it."

"It's a great family house. Not a lot of young families moving in to the Lomand area right now. It's been up for a while, and Randy was sure we would be successful. The inspection showed nothing, so it's ours." He grinned. "My kid and a house in one day. Halton is right—you're my lucky charm."

"I think you're mine."

He winked. "You know it."

## DOM

Today was Hannah's birthday, and Chase had arranged a surprise party for her. I was grateful for the activity to take my mind off next Saturday. Meeting my son. I worked at the garage in the morning, while Cherry ran some errands. Chase was keeping Hannah busy all day, bringing her to the bar later, where we would all be waiting. She was going to be surprised. Everyone would be even more surprised when Chase proposed. Cherry was excited for Hannah and thrilled she'd found someone to share her life with.

We kept our engagement low-key, but our friends knew. They were thrilled, and Hannah was so excited about the fact that her mom would be living a few minutes away from her. I had shared my news about Josh, and they were all supportive and understanding, knowing how nervous I was about seeing him and his reaction to me. Cherry had printed off a copy of the picture she'd taken, and it was clipped above the desk in the office. Seeing it filled me with emotions, both sad and happy. He looked like a great kid, and I hated that I had missed so many years with him, but I was pleased to see he looked fine.

"How does it feel, knowing a week from today, you'll be looking at him in the flesh?" Charly asked, sliding onto the stool beside me.

I met her curious gaze with a smile. "Scares the shit out of me that he'll find me lacking," I replied honestly. "Or that I won't have the patience to deal with him. I remember thirteen. I was a little bastard with an attitude."

Charly laughed, tilting her head back, her bright-red hair falling over her shoulders. "I think we all were. I thought I knew everything when I was a teenager." She rubbed my shoulder. "But you'll be fine, Dom. You'll have Cherry with you. It might be tough at first, but you'll figure it out." She smiled. "He's going to be nervous too."

I rubbed my face. "I know. I have no idea what lies she's been telling him all these years. He might hate me because she's taught him to."

Cherry walked in, hearing my last words. "Then we'll unteach him. You'll find common interests. He loves cars, he told me. Bring him here and let him see what you do. I bet that breaks the ice."

Charly nodded, looking enthused. "Great idea. He can see you in action. Watch the guys working. He'll have tons of questions, and you can talk to him about something he loves. That can be your bridge."

I rubbed my chin. "Good idea."

Charly and Cherry exchanged a knowing look, making me laugh. "You ladies are awesome."

Charly stood and sniffed. "Of course we are. I keep telling you that."

She hugged Cherry. "I'm so excited about tonight. Hannah is gonna be so surprised."

Cherry smiled. "I know. It's so hard not to call her and wish her a happy birthday, but I'm afraid I'll slip and say something. Chase has worked so hard to keep this a secret. Last night, I mentioned I was busy all day and would call her tonight. She probably thinks I've forgotten."

"She'll forgive you," I assured her.

Charly chuckled. "Yes, she will. What time are you heading to the bar to decorate it?"

"About three."

"Great. Maxx will stay with the kids, and I'll meet you there. Stefano's sister is coming to babysit all the kids tonight so we can all be there."

I laughed. "That's a handful."

"I know. But she insisted. Gabby says she's bringing her eldest daughter, who loves kids, so they'll be fine. I told them I'd have my cell on in case. And Mama Rosa would leave the party and help if needed," Charly added.

"Good plan."

"I'm not missing my boy getting engaged," she added.

"And Brett is flying home to be there. It's going to be an epic party."

I had to agree. Only a few of us knew about Brett flying in. Even fewer knew the reason he was coming. Chase was playing his cards close to his chest about the engagement. Charly was his closest ally, and she was in on the secret. To say she was thrilled with the way his life was going was an understatement. She loved Chase as if he were her own. She was his friend, pseudo-mother, and most trusted adviser wrapped up in a blunt, ferocious, tiny, redheaded package.

Charly left with a wave, and I looped my arm around Cherry. "Got everything you needed?"

"Yes. All the decorations and balloons, the cake, everything on Chase's list."

"He's going all out."

She smiled softly. "He loves her a lot."

I pulled her close. "I love you."

She kissed me. "I know."

"When you gonna marry me?"

Cherry rolled her eyes. "You only asked me a couple of weeks ago. How about we move, you get to know your son, then we'll talk about a date?"

"You want a big wedding?"

"No, that's for Hannah. I'd be happy with just us, a few friends, and a nice dinner."

"What about a honeymoon?"

She pursed her lips. "I'd rather spend the time at the house."

"A night in a fancy hotel first?" I asked. "Somewhere with a big tub where I can ravish you?"

Cherry laughed. "I could be persuaded."

I winked at her. "Prepare yourself then, woman."

She wrapped her arms around my neck. "Okay, then."

We danced together, Cherry beaming in delight. The party had gone well, Hannah surprised and overwhelmed. Chase's proposal had been heartfelt and romantic, and everyone had applauded loudly. He had been shocked and thrilled when Brett and Kelly had shown up. The evening had been a success.

"Mother and daughter engaged a few weeks apart," I murmured. "Not a usual occurrence."

Cherry laughed, her fingers tightening on my waist. "I suppose not."

"And engaged to friends."

She looked around the room, smiling at all the familiar faces. "I feel as if I got a new family," she admitted. "They're an amazing group."

I had to agree. "Charly encourages that atmosphere. I think it's astonishing." I bent and kissed her mouth. "If someone had told me a year ago I'd be holding the love of my life, getting married, and being given a new family, as well the chance to rebuild my relationship with Josh, I would never have believed them."

Cherry's lovely eyes were warm and filled with emotion. "The same goes for me. Hannah is well and happy. Working in a safe place. She's in love and getting married. I have a new job, a new place to live, and I get to do it with the sexiest man in the room." She paused. "One I love with all my heart and who I can't wait to share a life with."

I pulled her closer.

"A year ago, I was so alone. I hated so much of my life," she admitted softly. "I worried about Hannah constantly. I never thought the future held anything good for me. Until I met you." She laid her head on my chest, holding me tight. "I love you, Dominic Salvatore."

I pulled her into the corner, lifting her chin and kissing her. "I need to take you home now, Cherry G. Show you how much I love you."

She grinned. "Good idea."

I pulled her behind me, and we stopped to say good night to a few people. The party was winding down, and I knew Chase, Brett, Maxx, and Stefano would sit and catch up with one another. Charly and Gabby would pull their husbands away to their homes and children after a while. I needed Cherry alone now. No one looked surprised. We got hugs and promises to see one another the next day for an impromptu barbecue. We'd catch up with everyone then.

In the meantime, I had plans for Cherry.

And none of them involved much sleep.

By the following weekend, I was a nervous wreck. I was having trouble sleeping, worried and anxious. Cherry was patient, understanding my tension. Friday night, I sat on the sofa, unable to sleep. I left Cherry in bed and paced for a while before sitting down. I let my shoulders fall forward, weaving my fingers together on the back of my head, stretching the sore muscles. I startled when Cherry sat next to me, rubbing my back. She didn't speak, but offered me the comfort of her touch.

"What if he hates me?" I said, finally expressing my fears out loud. "What if she's poisoned him against me so much, I don't have a chance?"

"Then we'll un-poison him."

"What if he won't talk to me?"

"We'll find common ground."

"What if he refuses to see me again?"

"Then we'll wait. You can give Halton letters for him. This time, you'll know he gets them."

"I'm fucking frightened, Cherry."

"I know, sweetheart," she soothed. "But I'm here. We're going to get through this."

I kept hearing one word repeated in her calm assurances. *We*. It reminded me of one very big difference from the past.

I wasn't alone in this anymore.

Halton was in my corner.

And so was Cherry.

He was looking after the legalities, and she was handling all the rest.

*Me.*

I turned to her, meeting her calm gaze. She rested her head on my shoulder, and I wrapped my arm around her. "What would I do without you, Cherry G?"

"You don't have to find out."

I pulled her to my lap so she straddled me. I captured her mouth with mine, kissing her. Tasting her sweetness. Her love. The way she cared for me.

She made me feel important. Seen. She gave me the courage to do this, no matter the result. Because she would be there with me.

I deepened the kiss. I had been needy and physical with her all week. Taking her nightly, not always gentle. But right now, all I felt for her was love. Tenderness. The joy of knowing she was here and mine.

Our tongues slid together in a leisurely dance, igniting my desire. I slipped my hands under the loose T-shirt she wore, stroking her back. I glided my fingertips over the dips and curves of her spine, feeling the delicate bones that held such strength. I widened my hands, marveling at the silkiness of her skin. The roundness of her hips. The warmth of her neck. I cupped her ass, groaning when I realized she was naked under the shirt. I dipped lower, finding her heat. The slickness of her coating my fingers.

"You want me, baby?" I whispered, kissing my way up her neck and pulling at her lobe with my teeth, swirling my tongue on the sensitive skin behind her ear.

"Yes," she pleaded, grinding herself on my hard cock. "I need you."

"I need you too," I hissed as she tugged on the waistband of my boxers. I lifted my hips so she could push away the offending material and settle herself back on my thighs, her smooth skin rubbing on my coarser legs.

I kissed her again, holding her close, needing her heat to warm me. I tangled my hand into her thick hair, loving the feeling of her curls on my skin. I fisted the long locks, groaning in satisfaction as she gripped me, guiding me into her body. We both stilled as I slid in, our eyes locked, the connection between us growing stronger every second. Nothing compared to being inside her. Feeling her wrapped around me. The way her muscles gripped me tightly. The feeling of home in being so intimate with her. Never had I experienced a connection the way I did with Cherry.

She gripped my shoulders as she began to move. Slowly rolling her hips, holding me inside her body, taking me deeper. I grabbed her hips, guiding her. Needing to be as connected with her as possible. Our movements were slow. Gradual. Building. We never separated, moving together, holding each other. Close, always close. Our gazes locked in the dim light, her love blazing from her eyes. I knew mine met her passion with the same intensity. We didn't talk, our sounds filling the room. The creak of the sofa, the rubbing of the fabric around us. Her soft whimpers, my needy groans. Her name a breath from my mouth, mine whispered like a prayer from hers. I worshipped her the way she deserved to be worshipped, giving her everything I could offer with my body. I slipped a hand between us, teasing her clit, and she came, stiffening her spine and strangling my cock. I rode it out, wanting more from her. For her. I pulled her mouth back to mine, kissing her deeply. Capturing her oxygen and using it as my own. She returned my kisses with a passion that shocked me. Delighted me on every level. She began to move faster, her moans and whimpers getting louder. I wrapped an arm around her waist, the pleasure beginning to wind through my body. My balls drew up, color exploding behind my eyes as I orgasmed, locked inside her so deeply, I knew I was about to be blown away with pleasure.

I shattered, soaring high, not caring about the fallout. She screamed her release into my mouth, and we succumbed together, burning bright. Hot. Filled with love, desire, and, finally, completion. Never had I experienced such intensity. Never had an orgasm gone on so long.

Until we hit the ground.

Shivering, shaking, holding each other tightly.

Unable to speak. To move.

To try to explain what had just happened.

Because no words could properly express the intensity and emotion of it.

I pulled the blanket off the back of the sofa and draped it around us. We sat utterly motionless and silent, me still inside her, not wanting to move.

Until she cleared her throat.

"Wow."

I pressed a kiss to her head. "Wow is right."

"I'm not sure what that was. Aside from amazing."

"You took the words right out of my mouth."

She yawned, cuddling into my chest. "We should go to bed."

"Uh-huh."

"Do you think you could sleep now?"

"I'm not sure I can move."

"Then we'll stay here."

I chuckled. "That can't be too comfortable."

"I'm okay."

With a Herculean effort, I stood, not surprised to find my legs shook. "I need you to be more than okay."

"Don't trip on your underwear."

That made me laugh, and somehow, I kicked them off from my ankles, carried her to bed, and crawled in after her. She wrapped her arms around me, and I rested my head on her chest, listening to her heartbeat.

"I love you, Cherry."

I felt her smile.

"I know."

# CHAPTER FOURTEEN

## Dom

"What if she doesn't show?" I asked Halton.

He took a sip of his coffee, looking calm. "I'll call the judge, and he'll rain hellfire down on her." He indicated the chair beside him. "Sit. You're not fighting this on your own, Dom. I'm here to confirm the boy is here, and I'll stay across the restaurant to make sure she doesn't do anything to mess with your time. I'll report everything to the judge."

"Who is she bringing?"

He scoffed. "Her lawyer canceled this morning. So, I guess, no one." He looked past me. "They're here. Go sit with Cherry."

I headed to the table across the restaurant we'd agreed on. It wasn't busy, and the food was decent. Josh could pick out whatever he wanted, and I got to have lunch with my son for the first time in years.

They walked in, and I was surprised when, other than a scathing glance my way, Roxanne indicated me to Josh and listened to whatever Halton had to say with a nod. I heard her reply, her sharp "I'll be here at three," clear across the space. Then she left.

Halton walked over, and I stood, tamping down the tsunami of emotions I felt. Josh was tall for his age, and even if I hadn't seen a picture of him, I still would have known him. He looked like me. Right down to the serious expression I tended to wear. I could tell he wasn't overly happy to be here, but he came.

We stared at each other for a moment, then his gaze bounced to Cherry. "Hey, it's the math lady. What are you doing here?"

She smiled and held out her hand. "It's Cherry," she reminded him. "I'm your dad's fiancée."

"Oh." He frowned. "Is that why you were nice to me?"

"No. I didn't know who you were until you told me your name. I was nice to you because I liked you."

"Oh," he repeated. "Cherry, then."

His gaze swung back to me. "I'm not calling you Dad."

I held out my hand, not surprised at his words. "How about Dom? It's good to see you again, Josh."

He stared at my hand, then extended his. "I guess."

Halton lifted his eyebrows at me and nodded. "I'll be over there." He walked away, returning to his table and opening his laptop.

I indicated the booth where Cherry was sitting. "Will you join us?"

He sat down with a huff. "Like I have a choice."

I sat across from him, and we studied each other. "How about you give me a chance?" I asked. "It's lunch and a couple of hours."

"And next week for the whole day. Taking me away from my weekend."

"I've waited nine years for that day, Josh."

That seemed to surprise him. "Why?"

I rubbed my eyes. I didn't want to get into a mud-slinging match about what his mother had done, compared to what she had told him. I only wanted to get to know him. For him to know me.

"Because you're my son, and I missed you."

He frowned, and I had a feeling he wanted more. I looked at Cherry, feeling helpless and unsure how to answer.

"Why don't we take it one step at a time?" she suggested. "We'll concentrate on today. How about we order lunch, and you tell us about your life, Josh. Did the math tips I gave you help on your test?"

That simple question changed his countenance completely. He grinned at her. "Yeah, it did. It made studying easier, and I got a C+ on my test. Last one, I got a D. My teacher was happy, and my mom didn't yell at me."

"Good," she said, handing him a menu. "I can show you a couple more if you want."

"Okay." He studied the menu. "What can I order?"

"Whatever you want," I said. "I'm having a cheeseburger platter. With onion rings. I'm not a big fry guy."

Josh's eyes grew round. "Me too. I always get rings. And a chocolate shake."

"Good plan."

And he smiled.

It did something to me, seeing his smile directed at me. I returned it with one of my own, and Cherry laughed. "I'll have the same, but with fries." She winked at Josh. "He always steals a couple of fries from my plate. You can too if you want."

"Maybe a couple," he replied with a shrug.

I had to laugh. He looked and sounded like a thirteen-year-old me. Trying to seem cool and unaffected when everything was chaotic around me.

And I liked it.

Conversation between Josh and me was stilted, but when it came to Cherry, she could draw him out. When I asked him a question, his answers were short, but at least he spoke. I was worried I would get the silent treatment. Cherry was able to get him to talk about his love of baseball and football. That he enjoyed running. He wasn't into girls—yet. And he admitted he was a bit of a loner.

"We've moved a lot," he admitted, beginning to relax.

"Why is that?" I asked cautiously.

He shrugged. "Usually 'cause Mom has a new man, and we follow them." He rolled his eyes. "This one is a real winner."

I exchanged a look with Cherry. "You don't like him?"

"He's lazy and treats me like a baby. Plus, he yells a lot. I hate that."

"Ah," I murmured. "Do you feel unsafe?"

"No. He's just a jerk." He crunched an onion ring. "Cherry said her boyfriend was a mechanic. I assume that was you?" he asked. "You work on cars?"

"I do. I help run a garage. I work on cars and motorcycles and assist with restorations."

His eyes lit up. "Cool. What's your favorite?"

"I love vintage sixties. Restoring those is my favorite. I like the older bikes too." I paused. "We're working on one right now in the garage. Maybe you'd like to see it."

"Hell yeah." He swallowed. "I mean, heck yes."

Cherry chuckled, and I shook my head.

Josh grinned. "I'm not supposed to swear."

"I hear you," I replied. "Cherry keeps a swear jar. So does Charly. And her ears are like fine-tuned microphones. They pick up every one that happens in the garage."

"Who is Charly?"

I picked up my milkshake. "Well, let me tell you…"

Josh looked over my shoulder. "Mom is here," he announced, sounding almost disappointed.

I glanced at my watch. "Oh wow."

Time had flown past. Once we'd gotten on the topic of cars and the garage, Josh's demeanor had changed completely. He'd become engaged and interested. There was no attitude, only rapid questions, barely letting me answer before the next one was out of his mouth. He laughed and talked, no longer unhappy about being there with us. I forgot about our time limit, Halton in the corner, and everything else. There was simply my son and me with Cherry—sharing lunch and getting to know one another.

I stood, running a hand along the back of my neck, once again anxious. I wasn't sure what was going to happen now. Josh solved my dilemma by sliding from the booth and meeting my eyes. "So, next week, do you come pick me up or what?"

Cherry slipped her hand into mine. "We'll arrange it with Halton."

"What time?" He sounded so eager, I wanted to smile.

"Whatever time you want."

"I'm up at eight."

"I'll get Halton to arrange it with your mom."

"Can we go to the garage?"

"Absolutely," I said. "I'll introduce you to all the guys."

"And Charly?"

I laughed. "I couldn't keep her away if I tried."

"Maybe Rosa would make some food for lunch?" he asked.

"If I asked, she would." I grinned as he lifted an eyebrow. "So, I'll ask."

He studied me. "You're okay, Dom."

I grinned, almost giddy. "Thanks, Josh. I like you too."

He nodded. "Okay. So, I'll see you next week, right?" There was a look of worry on his face and in his voice. As if he needed reassurance.

I put my hand on his shoulder and squeezed. "Nothing will keep me away now, Josh."

He had exchanged cell phone numbers with Cherry and me. "I'll text you as soon as I know the time, and you can confirm with your mom."

"Great."

Cherry stepped forward. "May I give you a hug?"

He looked startled, then nodded. "Sure."

Cherry hugged him and smiled. "See you next week."

"Okay."

He turned to go, and I had to blink away the sudden moisture in my eyes. It shocked me when he turned back. "See you next week, Dom." Then he held out his fist.

I fist-bumped him and nodded. "Next week."

"Thanks for lunch. It was, ah, great to meet you."

I met his gaze. "The swing thing you told Cherry about? It was real, Josh. That was me. Us. And I hope one day you'll remember more."

He frowned, then began to smile. "I hope so too."

This time, I didn't hold back as he walked away. The tears rolled down my face, and I didn't care who saw me.

It had been an incredible day. I had lunch with my son, and he fist-bumped me. It was my first physical contact with him since he was a toddler. The sensation was overwhelming.

I pulled Cherry into my arms and held her.

"Thank you," I murmured.

"You're welcome. And it's just the beginning," she whispered.

I liked those words.

Halton showed up at the garage on Monday afternoon, Fee with him. My heart sank in my chest, and I hurried over, meeting him.

"What's wrong?"

He smiled, waving his hand. "Nothing big. We were driving back from a place I was thinking of buying and saw the sign for Littleburn, and I thought I'd drop in and see you."

"You know, Counselor, for a lawyer, you're a shit liar."

He chuckled.

Cherry came over, looking concerned. "What happened?"

"Honestly, nothing big. But I did hear from the judge today."

Cherry frowned. "Let's talk in the office."

We went in, and she shut the door. I grabbed her hand for support. "Tell me."

"We were driving by," Halton stressed. "Roxanne called the judge, furious you had Josh's cell number and could reach him directly, therefore circumventing her."

"He offered. I didn't think I was breaking any rules."

"You didn't. The judge thought it was a positive sign that Josh was open to exploring a relationship." Halton crossed his arms. "I guess he was a little enthusiastic about his upcoming visit to the garage, and she wasn't happy."

"I don't like the fact that Josh says her new boyfriend yells at him."

Halton's eyebrows shot up. "Good information to know. I can use that."

I released Cherry's hand and gripped my hair in frustration. "I'm not trying to destroy her relationship with Josh. Or interfere in his life. I want to be a part of it. Why is that so hard for her to understand? Why can't she give up on the grudge she has against me?"

Fee spoke up. "When I met Halton, I was getting a divorce. My husband no longer wanted me, but he didn't want anyone else to have me either. Lots of people are like that."

I barked out a laugh. "So, if I were single, miserable, and alone, she might be more open to me seeing Josh?"

Halton shrugged. "She strikes me as the type who wants all the attention and affection from every person in her life. She won't like the fact that Josh liked you and Cherry."

"Should I stay away for a while?" Cherry asked.

"No!" I said, panicked. I looked at Halton. "Right?"

"Absolutely not. But she is gonna try every trick in the book. She told the judge you were demanding the whole day from eight to well after dinner."

"Josh asked if I could get him at eight. I said we'd ask. And I never mentioned after dinner."

"I said as much. The judge is onto her, I think. He suggested nine to four. Then if it goes well, you get him the following weekend from nine Saturday morning to lunch on Sunday. We'll go from there."

"What should I do to protect Josh?"

"Exactly what you are doing. Putting him first and

letting him decide. Don't engage with Roxanne. If she comes after you, you call me."

He stood. "Now, my car is making a funny noise. Can you squeeze me in?"

I knew he was trying to distract me. I appreciated the fact that he'd come here to see me—to tell me face-to-face that Roxanne wasn't going to accept this quietly.

But this time, I wasn't going away so easily.

# CHAPTER FIFTEEN

## Dom

Saturday, Roxanne was waiting outside when I pulled up to get Josh. I was excited, nervous, plus worried she would pull something to stop it. I got out of the car, approaching the front door.

"Roxanne," I said mildly. "I'm here to get Josh."

"You're early."

I glanced at my watch. "It's three minutes to nine."

"He isn't ready."

The front door opened, and Josh came out, carrying a backpack. He seemed pleased to see me. "Hey, Dom. Cherry with you?"

"She's waiting in the car."

"Great." He leaned up and kissed his mom's cheek. "I'll see you later."

She watched him go, a frown on her face. She turned to me with a glare. "Keep your girlfriend away from him. He has a mother."

"Is that what's bothering you so much? First off," I said, "Cherry is my fiancée, and you have no say in her being around. Second, she isn't trying to take your place.

I'm not trying to usurp your position in his life. You're his mother. I have always respected that. But I'm his father, and I want to know him. You've stolen enough years from me."

"Maybe I'll move again."

I had to laugh. "Have you met my new lawyer? He'll stop you so fast, your head will spin. I'm here, and I'm not going anywhere. For Josh's sake, why don't you try to let us get along? It's better for him, and he is the only one I care about in this scenario. Not you. Not your relationship with him. Just him. He can have us both. Love us both." I shook my head. "Grow up, Roxanne. You don't have to work to be the center of his life. You already are. Let him have love from other people. No kid should be denied love."

Then I walked away before I said anything else.

I maintained a fake smile all the way to Littleburn. Josh asked a lot of questions, and Cherry kept up her information-gathering. She turned to high-five him when he told her he got a B+ in a pop quiz in math that week.

"Way to go!"

We stopped for breakfast, and as we waited for the pancakes, I slipped to the restroom and called Halton. I told him what happened, and for a moment, he was quiet.

"You didn't say anything wrong, Dom. You spoke your mind, and you were calm. I'm glad you told me, though. If she complains, I'll be able to defend it."

"I should have kept my mouth shut."

"I get it—sometimes it's hard. I think it'll be fine. Now, go enjoy the day with your boy."

I hung up and looked in the mirror. I splashed some cold water on my face and decided he was right. I had been looking forward to this all week. I wasn't going to let Roxanne and her petty demands ruin the day.

"Dom, what is that?"

I chuckled. "It's a computer we use to develop concepts for artwork on cars." I turned on the machine, showing Josh the program. "Stefano likes to draw by hand, then input it. Maxx likes the machine. I do a bit of both, but it's a hobby to me. Those two are the real artists."

He'd been full of questions from the moment we arrived. The guys all made sure to be here, and he'd talked to every one of them. He was in awe of Maxx's size. Stefano's talent pulling apart a car, Brett's sculpting of new parts, and Chase's leather work. He was fascinated by the Indian motorcycle in the corner, listening to the crew talk shop, and was thrilled when I had him help me with an engine we were rebuilding. Charly and Cherry came and went, and Gabby and Kelly stopped by to say hello. He was looking forward to when Rosa and Mack were coming, already in love with Rosa's food, even though he'd never tasted it.

"Mom's not much of a cook," he confided. "We eat the same stuff all the time."

I recalled her kitchen failures, and I was thrilled I could give him such a treat.

"You have so many people around," he said, sounding wistful. "It's awesome. Do they visit you too?"

"On occasion. And we do suppers and barbecues."

"That sounds like fun."

"Maybe you can join us. If you want," I added.

"For sure."

I had to turn so he didn't see my expression. I wanted to shout in excitement over his easy acceptance. His desire to be around.

"I need to tighten this," I said, indicating a part. "What do I need?"

"A socket."

"Size?"

He looked at the part, then my tools. "This one."

"Right." I handed him the tool. "You want to try?"

He took the wrench from my hand and did it perfectly.

"Great job, son. You're a natural."

"Mom says I have to be a businessman."

I shrugged. "I think you can make up your own mind when you're older."

"Are blue-collar workers really less important?"

I laughed, knowing where he'd gotten that idea. "Blue-collar workers are honest, hardworking people. And these days, they make as much, if not more, as some CEOs do. Make up your own mind about your future. Love what you do. That's the best advice I can give you."

"Do you love it?"

"Yeah, I do."

He looked around. "I think I already know, but I'll wait to tell Mom."

"Good plan."

Cherry strolled into the garage. "Lunch is ready."

Josh grinned. "I'm starving."

She ruffled his hair. "Good. Because between Rosa, Mary, Charly, and me, there's a feast at the house. And Hannah just got here."

"Your daughter? The cop?"

"That's her."

"Awesome!" He looked between us. "She's like the closest thing I would have to a sister, you know?"

And he was gone.

"Wash your hands before you eat!" Cherry called, then laughed. "I don't think he was listening. Too excited."

I stared at Cherry, who smiled. "I think he is settling in pretty fast."

"He is. Roxanne is gonna hate it."

Cherry shrugged. "Too bad. Let's go watch our kids bond."

I followed her eagerly, looking forward to seeing that.

Josh stuck close to Cherry, like a shadow. It made me laugh since he was taller than her, and hiding behind her did nothing. But I did love that he relied on her already. He sat next to her, staring at Hannah.

"You're a cop?"

"I am," she said. "So behave, or I'll cuff you."

His eyes grew big. "Really?"

Chase leaned over, grinning. "She will."

"Awesome."

Hannah chuckled. "You've got a lot of food on that plate. You gonna eat it all?"

"I've never seen so much food," he acknowledged. "I had to try it all. Dom talks about it all the time."

I ruffled his hair. "Not all the time."

Josh rolled his eyes. "When you're not mooning over Cherry or talking about one of the guys or how cool the girls are, you do."

Everyone laughed, including me. I had just been ratted out by my kid.

Josh tried a mouthful of lasagna, shutting his eyes as he chewed. He looked at Rosa, who was standing close. "That is the most delicious thing I have ever eaten."

She laughed, delighted, and patted his head. "You stick with me, little man. I make sure you get all the good food."

"I love this place," he muttered.

I chuckled and met Cherry's gaze. She leaned close, her lips next to my ear. "Mooning over me, Mr. Salvatore?"

I turned, pressing a kiss to her mouth. "Always, Cherry G."

She grinned, and I saw Josh watching us. I kissed her again. "Behave." I threw a wink his way, and he shook his head as if to tell me I was the one who had to behave. Then he turned to Hannah and started peppering her with questions about being a cop. Asking Chase about the interior he was working on.

"He is so bright," Cherry said. "Inquisitive about everything."

"I know."

"I think he and Hannah are going to get along just fine."

"He is staring at her like she hung the moon. I think introducing them might have given him something he's wanted for a long time."

Cherry laughed. "They're exchanging numbers. How cute."

"She gives hers up far easier than her mother did."

Cherry glanced sideways. "You are a lot more trouble than Josh will ever be. I was being cautious. And I was right. You're a thief."

"A thief?" I asked.

"Yes. You stole my heart."

I grinned and kissed her harder than I should with my son watching. But I didn't care. "I'm not giving it back either."

"Good."

The hours flew by, and all too soon, I was taking Josh back to Kingston. Cherry stayed behind to give us a chance to be alone.

"So, you okay to stay the night next week?" I asked.

"Yeah."

"Great. We bought a new house, and we're going to see

it again. You can come with us." I cleared my throat.
"Choose which room you'd like. We can paint it, and you
can pick out whatever furniture you want."

"Cool."

I glanced his way to see him staring at me.

"What?"

"Did you really walk away? When I was a baby?"

I drew in a deep breath. "That's a complex question,
Josh. But no, I didn't walk away. I wanted to be part of
your life."

"But Mom wouldn't let you."

I lifted one shoulder.

"She doesn't like other people much. She never lets me
go to friends' houses or do sleepovers."

"That must suck."

He nodded. "Sometimes. I can have friends over, but
she sticks around, so it's not much fun."

"Sometimes, Josh, people…well, people like your mom
have a hard time sharing."

He laughed. "You're a lot nicer when you talk about
her than she is when she talks about you. But you know
what?"

I pulled up in front of his house, putting the car in park
and turning to face him. "What?"

"I'm gonna make up my own mind about you. And
so far, I like you. You seem nice. And I really like
Cherry."

I smiled. "I know the feeling."

"Can I come to your wedding? I've never been to a
wedding."

"Absolutely."

The front door opened, and Roxanne stood on the
steps. She looked pointedly at her watch, and I wanted to
laugh. I was ten minutes early. But it had been a good day,

and I didn't want to ruin it fighting with her over a few moments.

"Your mom is waiting, Josh B'Gosh," I said, the old nickname I used to call him slipping out.

He paused before opening the door. "You called me that when I was little."

"Yeah, I did."

"I remember that."

He got out of the car, stopping before he shut the door. "Dom?"

"Yeah?"

"Can I, um, call you in the week? Or text you? Like, just to say hi?"

"Anytime. Day or night."

"Okay. Good. And I'll see you Saturday, right? At nine?"

"I'll be here."

He looked behind him. "Okay. Bye."

"Night, kiddo. See you soon."

Josh sent me a couple of texts on Monday and Tuesday, then there was nothing the rest of the week. Cherry told me he had sent her one on Tuesday and she had wished him well for a test he had on Wednesday, but he never replied.

"He's probably busy," she assured me. "He's a teenager."

I knew she was no doubt right, but when I arrived on Saturday to pick him up, I sensed a change in him. Roxanne hadn't bothered to come outside to goad me, for which I was grateful, but Josh's demeanor was unexpected.

He was quiet in the car, answering most of my questions with a grunt or a short yes or no.

"Cherry has breakfast," I said. "Then we'll head to the garage if you want."

"Sure," he replied, but not with the enthusiasm I expected.

"How was the test?"

He shrugged. "What I expected. I failed."

I frowned. "Maybe we can go over it, see if I can—"

He cut me off. "You're not my teacher. I don't need your help."

I bit back my retort, not wanting him to see me angry.

At the house, he greeted Cherry coolly, picking at his breakfast. She and I exchanged worried looks, and she tried to engage him in conversation. But his replies were short and, at times, dismissive.

After we finished, we began to clear the table.

"Josh," Cherry said. "Can you bring me some of the dishes, please?"

He frowned. "I'm not a servant."

She stopped what she was doing. "I beg your pardon?"

"I'm not here to work."

"I never said that. I asked you to bring me some of the dirty dishes."

"This isn't my home, and you're not my mom. I don't have to," he snapped and stomped off to the small room we'd made into a temporary bedroom.

I gaped at her. "What was that?"

"Him being a teenager."

"I don't like it. He shouldn't speak to you like that."

"I think he's a little tense today. Let it go."

I helped her clean the kitchen and went to get Josh to head to the garage. Part of me wanted to tell him unless he lost the attitude, we weren't going, but I hoped his mood would improve.

It didn't.

In the garage, he sulked and barely spoke. Showed no interest in the cars or what the guys were doing. He sat in the corner, playing on his iPad and slowly eating away at my patience. He was rude to Charly when she sat talking to him, and she looked at me with her eyebrows raised.

"Something is eating him," she observed, coming to stand beside me.

"He's been like this all day."

"Have you talked to him?"

"No." I rubbed the back of my neck. "His mom's boyfriend yells a lot. From what I gather, so does she. I don't want to add to it."

"You can speak firmly and not yell."

I sighed. "Can I, though? I tend to get mad fast."

She smiled. "It's amazing how we can control our temper for our kids. And he needs boundaries."

"Cherry said the same thing. She says he is pushing it today."

Charly chuckled. "She's right. Maybe things will go better once you show him the house."

I hoped so.

Josh looked around, clearly not impressed. "This is my room?" he asked.

"It will be when you visit, yes," I said. "You can pick a paint color and help paint it if you want. We'll do a painting party with everyone."

"When?"

"We get the house in two weeks. So, sometime after that."

"You plan on playing daddy every weekend?" he asked, a bitter tone in his voice. "Making me come here so you feel better, instead of letting me be where my friends are?"

That pushed me over the edge. I kept my voice low and firm. Calm. "Listen, Josh. I have no idea what flew up your butt this morning or the middle of last week, but knock it off with the attitude."

He narrowed his eyes at me. "What are you gonna do about it? Send me back to Mom?"

"What's going on? Where is this coming from? You're disrespecting Cherry, me, the guys in the garage. You were rude to Charly. That's not you."

"How do you know? You don't know me."

"I'm trying to. Which is more than you're doing right now. You're pushing me, all of us, away, and I want to know why."

"I don't want to talk about it." He tried to brush past me, but I put out my arm, stopping him.

"No. You're not leaving, and you're not burying your head in your iPad and ignoring me either. Talk to me."

"Why?" he shouted. "So I can get used to you being around, and then you're not?"

"I'm not going anywhere."

"For how long? Mom says as soon as you get tired of playing daddy, you'll walk again."

"I never walked!" I snapped. "Your mother took you away and refused to let me see you." I stepped closer. "I followed you to Saskatchewan. I tried to see you. I fought her as much as I could until I had nothing left to fight with. Every time I got enough money together, I tried again and failed."

"So, what changed?" he challenged, his voice no longer as hostile.

"Cherry did. She had a friend who listened to my story and helped. Halton found you and your mom and took on my case. He made my biggest dream come true."

He blinked. "I'm your biggest dream?"

"Yes. You're my son. I missed you so much, Josh. It felt as if part of me was gone."

"And you won't walk away?"

"Never."

He hung his head. "Mom and John told me all week not to get used to seeing you. That you'd leave again. That I meant nothing to you but a way to get back at Mom."

My anger was instant, as was my indignation. But I refused to let Josh be the punching bag for that anger.

I risked putting my hand on his shoulder and squeezing it. "They lied."

He looked up. "Sorry," he whispered.

"How about we start over? No attitude this time."

He sniffled, wiping his nose on his shirt sleeve. I didn't give him shit about it. "I really get a room?"

"Yep."

"Is Cherry mad at me?"

"No, but you owe her an apology. She isn't your mother, Josh, but she is my fiancée and will be my wife. She is part of my life, and you need to treat her with respect."

"Okay." He paused. "Thanks for not yelling."

I shut my eyes. "I don't want to yell at you, Josh. And you made me angry this morning, but I think talking is better than yelling. And it's better than sulking."

Cherry walked in, looking between us. "What's going on?"

Josh hurried over, surprising us both when he threw his

arms around her. "Sorry, Cherry. I was being a pain earlier."

She met my eyes as she hugged him. "We all have bad days, Josh."

"I'll do better."

She drew back and cupped his face. "You be Josh. We already think that is pretty awesome."

He nodded, and I heard his sniffle. Cherry hugged him again, letting him calm down a little.

"What do you think of your room?"

"It'll be great."

"What color do you want?"

"Blue. Can it be like a bright blue?"

"Let's go look at swatches," she said with a grin.

He smiled back, his good humor restored. "Okay."

I watched them leave, grateful we had gotten past the surliness, but wondering what other issues we would face.

# CHAPTER SIXTEEN

## Dom

Sunday, I followed him to the door, waiting until Roxanne answered. The rest of the visit had gone well, with no more outbursts. Josh was friendly and helped clean up after dinner. This morning, it had been fun to share breakfast with him. To see him when he first woke up. It reminded me of when he was young, his hair tousled, a sleepy smile on his face as he said good morning. The way he leaned into Cherry as she hugged him, as if seeking her embrace. It made my heart swell with hope for the future.

I was pleased when Josh high-fived me, then hugged me before he went inside. It was fast, and he was gone before I could return the gesture, but it was huge. Roxanne turned to go, but I halted her. "Wait."

Roxanne stared at me balefully. "What?"

"We need to talk."

She stepped out, her shoulders back, ready for a fight. "What?"

"Stop filling his head with lies. I never walked away,

and I'm not walking away this time. I want him in my life. You trying to sabotage it only makes you look bad. And your boyfriend. Tell him to stop raising his voice to Josh. He hates it."

She laughed. "You are so typical. You have no right to tell me how to raise my son. I—"

"*Our* son. Josh is our son, so it gives me the right."

"You think it's easy? Raising him?" She stepped closer. "What are your plans, Dominic? Play dad every weekend, holidays, and leave me with the rest? Make me the scapegoat for the weeks and responsible for everything else? Getting him to school, meeting with teachers, dressing and feeding him? And you get to be the fun one, having sleepovers and eating out?"

"I want him more than weekends."

She scoffed. "And how is that going to work? You live an hour away. You gonna drive him here to school every day? Pick him up? Take him to appointments? He isn't going to be living half time with you and half time with me and going to two schools, having two different lives. Have you thought about that?"

I had to admit, I hadn't thought that far ahead. I studied her, noting she looked tired. Not tired as in she didn't sleep well the night before, but weary. I took a deep breath and spoke calmly.

"Are you okay, Roxanne?"

My question surprised her, but she snapped back. "I'm fine."

"Surely we can come to a compromise where Josh gets the best of both of us, Roxanne. If we put him first and work together—"

She rolled her eyes and cut me off. "I'm not interested in playing friends with you. And I'm not moving to help you. You want him more? You change *your* life and prove how important he is."

Then she walked in and slammed the door.

Leaving me confused, worried, and upset.

With one huge question on my mind.

How was I going to do this?

## CHERRY

Dom was quiet when he got back from dropping off Josh. I'd expected him to be talkative and want to discuss how the weekend went. Instead, he stared out the window, paced the floor, and didn't say much except Josh was home safely.

"Roxanne looked really tired," he mused. "I texted Josh and told him to be nice to her."

"That was kind."

He shrugged. "Not sure why I did that."

"Because you're a good man."

He didn't reply, and he had been silent ever since.

"Dom," I began, waiting until he looked away from the window. "What is it?"

He sighed and leaned forward, resting his elbows on his thighs. "What am I going to do, Cherry?"

"About?"

"Going forward. I want Josh more. But how will that work? Me here, him there. He has a life, school. He can't live here part time and there part time."

"No, he can't." I paused. "But, Dom, you're jumping the gun a little, aren't you? You've only had him one weekend. Wait and see what happens."

Dom tapped his foot on the floor, the movement uneven and jerky. "I get the feeling he's lonely at times."

"He is, I think. It sounds as if his mom is a bit overbearing."

He snorted. "That's an understatement."

I regarded him fondly, reaching over and taking his hand. "Dom, I know you're a cut-to-the-chase kind of guy. You like action." I winked, trying to make him smile. "I should call you my bulldozer."

He huffed a little annoyed noise.

"But you need to take your time with this problem. Josh and his custody isn't going to happen overnight."

"I want to see more of him."

"I know. So talk to Halton and make a plan. But you can't expect it to happen immediately."

He sighed, shutting his eyes.

"Maybe we moved too fast," I said quietly.

"What?"

"If I weren't around, and we hadn't bought a house, you could move. Find a different job. See Josh easily."

He gaped at me. "Don't finish that."

"It's true." I drew in a deep breath. "We could simply put the house back up on the market. I could go live with Hannah for a bit. Or the apartment over the garage. You could go be with Josh."

"Not happening."

"Think about it, Dom. Without me in the picture, the solution would be so much easier."

He gripped my hand. "Without you, there is no solution. I love you, Cherry."

"He's your son."

He stared at me. "Would you leave me if the roles were reversed? If leaving me meant you could see Hannah more?"

"I would certainly give it consideration. And you should too."

"No. I refuse to believe there isn't a solution to this where I get both of you."

I stood, bending and kissing his forehead. He gripped my hips, stopping me from leaving. I cupped his face, fighting back my tears. "You have to consider it, Dom."

"I can't lose you."

"Your son is forever."

"So are we. If you want to sell the house, then you can come with me."

"Then I have to leave Hannah."

He stared at me. "So, we have to lose everything for our kids?"

"Maybe not. But if you chose Josh, I would understand." I smiled, even though I wanted to cry. "I'm going for a bath. I have a headache."

I walked away, glancing over my shoulder. Dom sat with his head down as if the weight of the world was on his shoulders.

I knew how he felt.

## DOM

Halton fit me in, and I sat across from him, telling him everything that had happened. What Cherry had said. What I was feeling. He listened, not interrupting. When I was done, he rested his chin on his steepled fingers, regarding me.

"Okay, first thing—Cherry is right. You're rushing here. You've had one sleepover. This will take time. Second, you're right. You can't have him half the time and divide his life between two cities. It's not fair to him, and no judge would grant that."

"So, I have to move if I want more custody?"

Halton was silent for a minute. "Where is Cherry, Dom?"

"She didn't want to come. She wants me to make this decision on my own. She says not to figure her into the equation."

He lifted his eyebrows. "Incredibly brave of her."

"I feel as if I'm already losing her."

"Not if you sit back and look at this rationally. With your head, not your heart."

"Explain that to me."

"Move ahead with your life. Let Josh be *part* of it. We'll request extended visits, but nothing that causes Josh upheaval."

"Such as?"

"You get him Friday evening until Monday morning. You pick him up after school and have him back there on Monday. You get three nights, two days. An extra day on long weekends." He met my gaze. "That's way more than you had before."

He was right. It was.

"You get to attend parent-teacher meetings. Go to school events. You make him a priority, not your entire life."

"What if he wants to live with me? I read a case recently—"

Halton held up his hand. "I know. That was the States. Canada's laws are different. A child is considered a minor until eighteen. He can't choose to live with you if his mother doesn't agree."

"Damn."

Halton chuckled. "Cherry was right about something else. You are a bulldozer."

I had to laugh. "I suppose." Then I grew serious. "I don't want to lose either of them, Halton."

"Then listen to me. Give this a little time. I'll put together a proposal to ask for more visitation. Request another meeting and present it to the judge. But not immediately. You still have to prove to him you're reliable. So we have to give it some time. You have to understand that."

I didn't argue, because I knew he was right. I knew Cherry was right. I was rushing everything.

"I know. I was…" I shrugged, lost for words.

"You were acting like a father who has missed his child. I get it, Dom. We'll do this correctly and by the book. Work with the system. Show the judge how cooperative you're being. How happy Josh is with you in his life." He sighed, rubbing his eyes. "But prepare yourself for Roxanne to fight. We'll fight back. The fact that he is doing better in school because of Cherry and her math teaching? That is gold. Keep that up."

I blew out a long breath, my chest loosening. Halton was right. I was jumping too far ahead. I had let my emotions get the best of me.

"Okay. I'll let you do your thing, and I'll keep going forward with my life and Cherry. Adding Josh to it, not letting that take over."

He nodded in agreement. "Yes. And get some sleep. You look like death warmed over. Go to Littleburn and talk to Cherry. Take her to dinner, talk to her, then take her home and *reassure* her." He winked drolly. "This must be hurting her as well."

I hadn't slept the night before, and Cherry had avoided me at the garage all morning. She looked as tired as I felt.

When I'd told her about meeting with Halton, she had nodded but refused to accompany me. Her words "take me out of the equation," echoed in my head the entire drive in.

That was unacceptable. She was the constant in the entire equation. The equalizer. I needed her, even more than I realized.

"I will."

I found Cherry at the garage. It was late, but she was at the desk, her head bent over, studying a form. She had her air cast off, resting her arm on a pillow. Her lips moved as she read soundlessly, her glasses perched on the end of her nose. She looked pale, but still so beautiful, it made my chest ache. The thought of losing her caused a pain I knew I wouldn't ever recover from.

I knocked on the doorframe, and she looked up. "Oh. Hi."

I walked in and shut the door behind me. I pulled out the flowers from behind my back and handed them to her. Her eyes widened, and I bent, cupping her face. I kissed her, sliding my tongue in and twisting it with hers. She tasted of coffee and chocolate, and I knew she'd been nibbling. It was another one of her nervous habits.

I pulled back, resting my forehead on hers. "I'm sorry, baby. I wasn't listening. You were right."

"I was?"

"Yes. And it's you and me, Cherry. We're together, and nothing is changing that, you understand?" I stood straighter, holding her cheeks. "I love you. I need you. You are my world, and we'll figure out Josh and how we all fit together, as a family. We'll do that together. You hear me?"

Her eyes filled with tears. "Yes."

"Then let's go home. I need you alone so I can show you how much I love you. And I have to feed you."

"In that order?"

"Whatever order you want, as long as we're together."

"Okay then, Dom. Take me home."

"Let's go."

# CHAPTER SEVENTEEN

## Dom

I spent a month doing exactly what Halton told me to do. I didn't argue with Roxanne. I picked Josh up on Saturdays and had him back at lunch the next day. We spent time at the garage. As a family. He helped us paint, enjoying the camaraderie of the crew as they gathered, once again helping one another. Charly and Cherry took him to choose furniture for his room, and he came back excited about having a double bed and a big dresser. They'd even bought sheets and a comforter, and he showed me the checked blue-and-black plaid, proud to tell me he'd picked it out himself. He was excited to be with us the day we got the keys and moved in, carrying in boxes with the rest of "the guys." Sitting and eating pizza afterward. Joking and laughing. Stefano let him have a sip of beer, and the comical face he made when he tasted it had everyone laughing. He decided to stick with soda.

Unable to sleep, I wandered the new house. Cherry was down for the count, exhausted. We had bought new furniture since neither of us had any, and the beds and sofa had been delivered. Mary gave us an extra table and chairs, so we had a place to eat. Chase and Hannah brought over all of Cherry's boxes, and she had put them in an empty room to unpack as we settled in. I checked on her, smiling at how right it looked to see her in our new room. Even devoid of much furniture aside from the bed, it looked like home, because she was there. I peeked in on Josh, surprised to find him awake. He was normally out fast, but he was propped up against his new headboard, the small lamp on his nightstand casting a glow in the room.

"You okay?" I asked.

"Can I ask you something, Dom?"

I stepped into his room and sat on the bed. "Anything."

He fiddled with his comforter, looking upset.

"What is it?"

"I keep remembering things. Like the swing. Did we go to the beach once?"

"A few times. You loved the water. I used to have to drag you out of it to eat a sandwich." I laughed as a memory hit me. "Once, I gave up, and we sat in the water, eating your favorite—peanut butter and banana sandwiches—and you dropped it into the water and plucked it out and ate it anyway, sand and all, before I could stop you. Your mother gave me shit about that for days," I said with a chuckle. "I put the umbrella over you, and you played in the water for hours with your trucks and pail. Ate your snacks there, everything. You cried so hard when it was time to go."

"We never go to the beach now," he said.

"We can. Summer is coming."

"You have a meeting with Mom and the judge next week. She told me."

I met his gaze. "I'm asking for more time with you, Josh. If you want that."

I explained Halton's idea and let him think about it. "If every weekend is too much, I understand. I know you must miss spending time with your friends—"

He interrupted me. "Not really. I see them at school, and Mom isn't big on having them over. I told you that before. I like coming here." He paused. "I like Cherry."

"She is pretty awesome."

He played with his comforter again. "I like you too," he said softly.

"Good. I like you a lot, Josh. I know you're not ready to hear that I love you, but you're my son, and I do."

For a moment, there was silence. "Did you really try to find me? You didn't forget about me the way Mom said?"

"I never forgot about you—not for a single day."

He frowned, and I stood. "Just wait a moment."

I left the room and returned with the small box Halton had given back to me. I handed it to him, and he opened it, looking at the envelopes.

"What is it?" he asked.

"Every letter and card I sent you that was returned. And ones I wrote and never sent since I didn't know where you were."

"There're so many."

"One for every birthday and Christmas. Plus some others."

"You kept them?"

"I always hoped I could give them to you one day."

"Can I read them?"

"They're yours."

He flicked through a couple envelopes. "I don't know where to start."

"Why don't you keep them for a while, then decide. I can put them in your closet, and when you're ready, they'll be waiting."

He paused, then opened one, scanning the childish card and chuckling over the twenty-dollar bill inside. He traced the "Love, Daddy" at the bottom.

"I always liked trucks," he said.

"I know."

He tucked the money back into the box but put the card on his nightstand. "Thanks," he said. "I think I'll open them one at a time."

"Sounds good." I took the box and slid it into his closet. "You gonna sleep now?"

"Yeah. Night, Dom."

"Night."

"Dom?" he called as I got to the door.

"Yeah?"

"I'd like to be here more, so I'll talk to Mom, okay?"

"Whatever you want. Any time I get with you is a bonus."

He grinned. "I think so too."

I sat with Halton, the judge, and Roxanne. I was surprised not to see her lawyer. I was even more shocked when she asked to speak. The judge nodded, and I braced myself for her words. She looked directly at me.

"Josh wants to spend more time with you. I'll agree to the extended visitation. No fighting."

"Why?" The word was out of my mouth before I could stop it.

She sighed. "Because I see the difference in him. He's happier. Doing better at school. Him coming for the weekends works for now, but it isn't a permanent solution."

"I know. We can address that at a later date. I just want to know my kid, Rox." The nickname I used to call her slipped out without thinking. It surprised me. It surprised her.

For the first time, she met my eyes, no hatred blazing from them. She looked resigned. Weary.

"And you should. Regardless of how awful we were, you were always a good dad. I remembered how good you were when I saw your text to Josh telling him to be nicer to me because I looked tired. I had yelled at you, yet you were kind."

I sat back in amazement.

She cleared her throat. "There is something else. I'm sick."

"Sick?"

"I have cancer. I start chemo next week. There may be times I need, ah, help."

"What about John?"

She rolled her eyes. "He walked. He said he didn't need a sick woman and a pesky teenager. So, it's just Josh and me."

"I'm sorry," I said sincerely. "Whatever I can do to help, let me know. We can take him or come help. Whatever you need."

"You mean that," she said incredulously. "After everything, you mean that."

"You're his mother. He needs you."

"Thank you." She turned to the judge and Halton, who was watching her with narrowed eyes. "Give me whatever paperwork you need me to sign. I won't fight it. I fired my lawyer, and I just want to make sure Josh is okay."

"I can draw up the papers," Halton said.

"I want it clear that if anything happens to me, Dom gets full custody."

"I'll make sure of it. I can recommend a decent lawyer for you as well."

"I don't think I need one. I'm done fighting this. I have something bigger to take on."

I met her eyes. I no longer saw the bitter, angry woman who took away my son. I saw the scared, lonely person who was facing the biggest battle of her life. Who needed to be okay so my son would be all right.

"And we'll be there to help you."

Friday afternoon, I was getting ready to pick up Josh. I walked out of the garage, frowning when I saw Cherry, Charly, and Gabby loading up the trunk and back seat.

"What are you doing?"

Cherry smiled at me. "We were cooking for Roxanne. We made a bunch of easy meals for her and Josh. Individual ones, so if she isn't hungry, Josh can heat up his own dinner. And we did some shopping, so she doesn't have to worry about that."

I marveled at the giving hearts of these women. As soon as I told them about Roxanne being ill, they had gone into helpful mode. Planning things for Josh. And, apparently, Roxanne.

I pulled Cherry close and kissed her brow. "Thanks, Cherry G."

"I'm coming with you."

"Okay."

We were quiet on the drive, and when we arrived, Roxanne was shocked as we walked in, carrying the meals and groceries. She was speechless, but when I brought in the second armful, she was talking to Cherry, the two women once at such odds, finding common ground—Josh's welfare.

When we left, it was the first time I didn't feel her

anger. Josh was curious. "So, you're not fighting with Mom anymore?"

I knew she hadn't told him yet. She wanted to have all the information before she shared.

"Your mom and I came to an understanding."

He looked pleased. "Good. So, I get all of you? I can like everyone, and no one is going to be upset?"

I took Cherry's hand. "Absolutely."

"And John is gone. I can come on the weekends and Mom said maybe the occasional night."

"Yep."

"I like this."

"Good."

Later that summer, Josh's laughter echoed from the water. He was splashing and playing with Theo and Thomas, once again a little kid himself. He still loved the beach, and we came as often as we could. Cherry chuckled beside me, reaching for my hand. Our friends were scattered around us, and not far away, Roxanne observed our son, a smile on her face. We often asked her to join us, and now that she was done with chemo, she said yes, enjoying the sun and the company. We would never be close or best friends, but we had come to an understanding. Josh wasn't a weapon she used to punish me with anymore.

She had moved to Lomand, living a few streets away from us, and now I saw Josh all the time. He was with us every second week, and he would go to school in the fall and be able to travel between the two houses easily. If Roxanne was having a bad week or day, he stayed with us. I loved having him around, and he loved being with us. Hanging out in the garage. Learning. Always learning. He was a natural with engines and cars and soaked up knowledge like a sponge.

I laced my fingers with Cherry's. "Okay there, baby? You have enough sunscreen on?"

She chuckled. "You were very thorough, Mr. Salvatore."

I grinned. "Can't have you all burned for the wedding."

She smiled back. "A week from today, I'll be your wife."

I lifted our joined hands and kissed her knuckles. "I can hardly wait."

We had a small celebration planned. Her and me. Hannah and Josh beside us. A party in the backyard with our friends. Neither of us wanted a big ceremony or reception. Hannah and Chase would be doing that shortly. We simply wanted to get married and go forward with our life.

"Hannah Banana!" Josh shouted. "You came!"

"Josh B'Gosh!" she yelled back. She had adopted my old nickname for him, and he loved it. He loved everything about her.

I snickered at the two of them and their pet names. They got on like a house on fire. Hannah adored her "little bro," as she called him, and he worshipped her. He loved sleepovers at her place or when she'd pick him up after school for ice cream.

"Dad!" he yelled. "Hannah Banana is here! We wanna race!"

I was still getting used to him calling me Dad. It had happened one day while we were at the garage. I was working on a car and asked him for a socket wrench. He handed it to me casually.

*"There you go, Dad."*

*I lifted my head so fast I almost hit the hood. I met his wide eyes.*
*"What?"*

*He cleared his throat. "Dad. That's okay, right?"*

*I had to blink. "Absolutely."*

*"Okay."*

*I lowered my head, not wanting him to see how emotional I was*
*feeling. "Okay."*

I stood, brushing off my legs. "I'm being summoned."

Cherry laughed. "Off you go, *Dad*." She knew how much I loved hearing him call me that.

I headed to the water with a grin. I looked around me.

Friends. Family. My son.

He was surrounded with love. So was I.

The sun was warm, the water cool, and life was good.

And I couldn't ask for anything more.

# EPILOGUE

## Three years later

## DOM

**H**appy birthday to you!!

The last line was loud and boisterous, everyone singing at the top of their lungs.

Josh grinned at the group, catching my eye and rolling his. He pretended to be embarrassed, but he loved it.

All our friends and family were there. The food was abundant, the tables almost groaning with the platters and dishes. Center spot was Rosa's lasagna—still Josh's favorite. Rosa and Mack were pseudo-grandparents for Josh. Maxx, Charly, Stefano, Gabby, Brett and Kelly, his aunts and uncles. Hannah and Chase were his adopted siblings. Especially Hannah. The two of them were incredibly close. Mary was another grandparent, always spoiling him. And all the kids were his cousins and friends. They all got along, despite the differences in their ages—the older ones looking out for the young. It was a great group, and we were blessed to be part of them.

Josh's mom had passed two years ago, cancer winning

the battle, although she had fought valiantly. We had found a plateau in our relationship and coexisted well, Josh our main focus. The last months of her life were spent happily, always included in anything to do with our son. Even Christmas. She was no longer bitter and angry, having found some sort of peace within herself. I was glad her last months on earth were content and she passed knowing Josh would be cared for. He had grieved hard, acting out on occasion, but everyone was patient with him, and he found himself again.

I smiled as he hugged Cherry, towering over her. He had a new name for me, and she was, of all things, Mumsy. I knew Mom was out of the question, but one day, he'd simply called her Mumsy, and when I looked at him quizzically, he had shrugged.

*"Cherry isn't right anymore. She's more than that. Mumsy fits her. Just like Dad-D fits you."*

*"Dad-D?" I questioned.*

*He grinned. "Yeah. I like it. You sound cool."*

And from that day on, it was Mumsy and Dad-D. We both loved it. It was the way he said the names. Affectionately, while rather teasing. It suited him and us.

He had grown, now over six feet tall. Thanks to Maxx and the guys, he loved to work out, so he was muscular, although still lanky. He was growing into his body as well as his brain. He was clever and still inquisitive. He loved to read, and his favorite spot to be was in the garage. He had promised his mom to think about the future carefully and had informed Cherry and me that he planned on taking some business courses, as well as training to be a mechanic. We would support him in every way possible. The life insurance that came to him after Roxanne passed was in an account, slowly accruing interest, and would cover his education. I knew she would be thrilled about that.

He leaned over, blowing out the candles. Sixteen. My son was sixteen.

Cherry looped her arm around my waist. "How did this happen?" she murmured.

I chuckled. "We're getting old, Cherry."

She elbowed me. "Speak for yourself, Dad-D."

I laughed, leaning down to kiss her cheek and whisper in her ear. "You know I love it when you call me Daddy."

She elbowed me again, color flushing her cheeks. It amused me that after all our time together, and the things we'd done, I could still make her blush.

"I'll show you old later," I warned. "Josh is going out with his friends. I'll have you all to myself. Maybe we can skinny-dip again."

She laughed. The house had changed a lot since we'd moved in. We'd renovated to suit us, and Josh had the entire basement decked out, with a huge TV and gaming console, as well as his computers. It was constantly filled with his friends. Upstairs, we'd gutted the kitchen and opened some walls. Outside, there was a large deck, and we'd added a pool, which was another draw for the kids. We loved hosting and having everyone over. Cherry especially loved having our grandkids spend the night to give Hannah and Chase "a break"—whether they asked for it or not. Their two children were spoiled rotten by my wife, but they were good kids and we enjoyed having them around. Maxx had three kids, the youngest a huge surprise. Stefano had three as well, and Brett had one child, so it was always a houseful when everyone was around, and the pool was well used.

"I don't think I want to risk it," she replied.

Josh had found us one hot summer night, skinny-dipping and frolicking in the pool, thinking we were alone. But he had decided to come home and caught us. He had been embarrassed beyond measure, and Cherry had never let us try it again. I had found it funny, but it seemed I was the only one.

"Come on, Cherry. Live dangerously."

She shook her head, walking away. "Josh's birthday gift is enough danger for me, thank you very much."

Josh's ears perked up. "Birthday gift? Dangerous? Did you get me a kit to make my own fireworks?"

I laughed, tilting my head to the driveway. "Come with me."

The guys followed me, knowing what was waiting. Josh frowned at the tarp-covered item. "Your old boat?"

I chuckled. "Nope. Got rid of that. Check it out."

Chase and I flipped up the tarp, and I watched Josh's face change from confused to elated.

"Dad!"

I grinned, running my hand over the vehicle. To an unknowing eye, it looked like a hunk of old metal. But Josh knew exactly what it was.

The start of his dream car.

He touched the metal reverently. "A sixty-nine Cobra," he breathed out. "How did you find it?"

"Through some contacts. It's straight as an arrow. Hardly any rust, and we even have some original parts. It'll take time, but we'll rebuild it. You can work on it yourself, make it yours. By the time you get your license, we should have it ready."

He stared at it. "It's incredible." He went around shaking everyone's hand and exchanging fast, backslapping hugs. He stopped in front of me and encased me in a bear hug.

Hugs for the girls were normal. For the grandparents. He hugged Cherry a lot. Ours were rarer. Always brief. But this one was different. Longer. Harder. Emotional.

"Thanks, Dad," he whispered.

"You're welcome." I expected him to release me, but he held on tighter, and I gripped him close as he continued to talk.

"For everything. For never giving up on me. For loving me when I wasn't ready to love you back. But I do. I love you, Dad."

He'd never said it before. He was fond of me. We were great friends. But it was the first time he'd ever said those words. Tears filled my eyes, and I held him tight. "Love you right back."

He eased back, wiping his eyes. "How does Mumsy feel about the car?"

"Like asking your father to put something in it so you can never go more than forty," Cherry replied, smiling at us, tears in her eyes, having witnessed our moment.

Josh grinned and swooped down, kissing her cheek and hugging her tight. "Sorry, no can do. Man, I can hardly wait to start!"

He turned and yelled. "Hannah Banana, did you see my car?"

"That hunk of metal?" she responded cheekily.

"Hey," he protested. "I am going to be so cool in that car once it's done."

She scoffed, pulling him into a headlock. "It'll take more than a car to make you cool, Josh B'Gosh."

They wrestled with each other, laughing.

I smiled at them, slipping my arm around Cherry.

"Good day," she said softly.

"Amazing," I agreed. "Thanks to you."

"Me?"

I turned, pulling her into my arms. "I took a job at a garage, hoping to find a good crew. Because of you, I found my life. My son. My heart. It's all you, Cherry. All of it."

She smiled up at me. "Right back at you, Mr. Salvatore."

I bent and kissed her. "Ready to go and finish celebrating?"

She grinned. "Yes. When they leave, we might need that dip. I'm suddenly feeling warm."

My smile was wide.

"Let's go, then."

Thank you so much for reading FULL THROTTLE. If you are so inclined, reviews are always welcome by me at your retailer.

This was a delightful series to spend time writing. I will miss the gang in Littleburn, ON Canada. Maybe one day I will revisit them.

If you love a growly hero, Richard and Katy VanRyan's story begins with my series The Contract. You meet an arrogant hero in Richard, which makes his story much sweeter when he falls.

If romantic comedy is your favorite trope, Liam and Shelby, from my novel Changing Roles, would be a recommended standalone to read next. It is a story of friends to lovers set in the bright lights of Hollywood.

Enjoy meeting other readers? Lots of fun, with upcoming book talk and giveaways! Check out Melanie Moreland's Minions on Facebook.

Join my newsletter for up-to-date news, sales, book announcements and excerpts (no spam). Click here to sign up Melanie Moreland's newsletter or use the QR code below

Visit my website www.melaniemoreland.com

Enjoy reading! Melanie

# ACKNOWLEDGMENTS

So many people were part of this journey.

Some were there from the start, others joined later.

But all are appreciated.

My hype team—thank you for all you do.

Minions—you rock my world.

George and Atlee, you are such gifts. We are lucky to have you with us.

Darlene, Daisy, Beth, and Deb. Thank you for all you do and your support. Your input makes my books better.

Lisa—words made us friends. I love that. And you.

Karen—a friend, a confidante, a right hand, and a little ball of fury all rolled into one. And you're all mine. Love you so much. And although the words are inadequate —thank you.

And Matthew—my greatest blessing and the reason I can do this. Love is not a big enough word for you. For us.

# ALSO AVAILABLE FROM MORELAND BOOKS

**Titles published under M. Moreland**

**Insta-Spark Collection**

It Started with a Kiss

Christmas Sugar

An Instant Connection

An Unexpected Gift

Harvest of Love

An Unexpected Chance

Following Maggie

The Wish List

**Titles published under Melanie Moreland**

**The Contract Series**

The Contract (Contract #1)

The Baby Clause (Contract Novella)

The Amendment (Contract #3)

The Addendum (Contract #4)

**Vested Interest Series**

BAM - The Beginning (Prequel)

Bentley (Vested Interest #1)

Aiden (Vested Interest #2)

Maddox (Vested Interest #3)

Reid (Vested Interest #4)

Van (Vested Interest #5)

Halton (Vested Interest #6)

Sandy (Vested Interest #7)

## Vested Interest/ABC Crossover

A Merry Vested Wedding

## ABC Corp Series

My Saving Grace (Vested Interest: ABC Corp #1)

Finding Ronan's Heart (Vested Interest: ABC Corp #2)

Loved By Liam (Vested Interest: ABC Corp #3)

Age of Ava (Vested Interest: ABC Corp #4)

Sunshine & Sammy (Vested Interest: ABC Corp #5)

Unscripted With Mila (Vested Interest: ABC Corp #6)

## Men of Hidden Justice

The Boss

Second-In-Command

The Commander

The Watcher

The Specialist

## Men of the Falls

Aldo

Roman

## My Favorite

My Favorite Kidnapper

My Favorite Boss

## Reynolds Restorations

Revved to the Maxx

Breaking The Speed Limit

Shifting Gears

Under The Radar

Full Throttle

## Standalones

Into the Storm

Beneath the Scars

Over the Fence

The Image of You

Changing Roles

The Summer of Us

Happily Ever After Collection

Heart Strings

# ABOUT THE AUTHOR

NYT/WSJ/USAT international bestselling author Melanie Moreland, lives a happy and content life in a quiet area of Ontario with her beloved husband of thirty-plus years and their rescue cat, Amber. Nothing means more to her than her friends and family, and she cherishes every moment spent with them.

While seriously addicted to coffee, and highly challenged with all things computer-related and technical, she relishes baking, cooking, and trying new recipes for people to sample. She loves to throw dinner parties, and enjoys traveling, here and abroad, but finds coming home is always the best part of any trip.

Melanie loves stories, especially paired with a good wine, and enjoys skydiving (free falling over a fleck of dust) extreme snowboarding (falling down stairs) and piloting her own helicopter (tripping over her own feet.) She's learned happily ever afters, even bumpy ones, are all in how you tell the story.

Melanie is represented by Flavia Viotti at Bookcase Literary Agency. For any questions regarding subsidiary or translation rights please contact her at flavia@bookcaseagency.com facebook.com/authormoreland

x.com/morelandmelanie

instagram.com/morelandmelanie

bookbub.com/authors/melanie-moreland

amazon.com/Melanie-Moreland/author/B00GV6LB00

goodreads.com/Melanie_Moreland

tiktok.com/@melaniemoreland

threads.net/@morelandmelanie

Printed in the USA
CPSIA information can be obtained
at www.ICGtesting.com
LVHW011104050624
782327LV00002B/333